Shannon's heart pounded in her chest and her insides had all but turned to mush.

For a few seconds there, when their conversation had paused, she could have sworn Rory was going to slide his hand behind her neck and pull her forward so he could kiss her.

Kiss her!

What a crazy thing to think! Ridiculous wishful thinking on her part, that's what it was. They might be having fun with his daughter, but that was no reason for a man to kiss a woman. She was simply too much of a romantic.

But figuring all this out now was actually a good thing. Rory had come right out and said that if he married again, he would want kids. His own kids.

And didn't that sound painfully familiar? She wasn't sure she could handle that kind of rejection again. So she was glad they'd had this little talk early on. There'd be no more wishful thinking. No more hoping he'd kiss her.

But right here and right now, she was a lonely woman, and she had both Rory and his daughter in her yard, enjoying her company. She'd be crazy to be upset. Crazier still to withdraw just because there couldn't be anything romantic between her and Rory. No matter what he said or how busy he was, someday he'd want to remarry. He'd want that family. Those kids.

And she couldn't have any.

Dear Reader,

After the year spent working on books about three brothers forming a rather large, rather noisy family, it was a culture shock to write only child Shannon Raleigh's story.

It seemed everybody in Shannon's life deserted her. Her husband left her. Her parents retired and moved out of town. And suddenly she was back in her hometown, running the family department store, with orders to sell it. She couldn't even get cozy with her neighbors or employees. As soon as she sold the store, she had to leave.

Enter Rory Wallace. He seemed to be Shannon's opposite. His wife might have left him, but his parents loved him and he has a brother and a sister…and a daughter. Though Finley the Diva is a bit hard to discipline on occasion, she's actually a lovable little girl…with a problem. She doesn't like Christmas because her mom left on Christmas Day two years before.

Can a woman who only wants a little companionship while she prepares for the holiday actually heal the hearts and souls of two wounded people, who don't even realize they're as lonely as she is?

I hope you like this story. I sprinkled it with lots of holiday fun, Christmas cookies and the wonder of seeing Christmas for the first time through the eyes of a little girl.

Susan

SUSAN MEIER

Kisses on Her Christmas List

TORONTO NEW YORK LONDON
AMSTERDAM PARIS SYDNEY HAMBURG
STOCKHOLM ATHENS TOKYO MILAN MADRID
PRAGUE WARSAW BUDAPEST AUCKLAND

Recycling programs for this product may not exist in your area.

ISBN-13: 978-0-373-74138-0

KISSES ON HER CHRISTMAS LIST

First North American Publication 2011

This edition published by arrangement with Harlequin Books S.A.

For questions and comments about the quality of this book please contact us at Customer_eCare@Harlequin.ca.

www.Harlequin.com

Printed in U.S.A.

Susan Meier spent most of her twenties thinking she was a job-hopper—until she began to write and realized everything that had come before was only research! One of eleven children, with twenty-four nieces and nephews and three kids of her own, Susan has had plenty of real-life experience watching romance blossom in unexpected ways. She lives in western Pennsylvania with her wonderful husband, Mike, three children, and two over-fed, well-cuddled cats, Sophie and Fluffy. You can visit Susan's website at www.susanmeier.com.

Books by Susan Meier:

THE BABY PROJECT*
SECOND CHANCE BABY*
BABY ON THE RANCH*

*Babies in the Boardroom trilogy

Other titles by this author available in ebook

For my friend Denise.

CHAPTER ONE

SHANNON RALEIGH turned to get a look at herself in the full-length mirror in the bathroom of her executive office suite and gaped in horror. The tall black boots and short red velvet dress she wore exposed most of her legs and the white fur-trimmed *U* at the bodice revealed a sizable strip of cleavage.

"I can't go into a roomful of kids dressed like this!"

Even from behind the closed door, she could hear her assistant Wendy sigh heavily. "Why don't you let me be the judge of that?"

"Because I know you'll say I look fine, when I don't. I can't usher kids to Santa's lap in a skirt so short I can't bend over."

"So don't bend over." Another sigh. "Look, Shannon, it doesn't matter that you're eight inches taller than Carlie. There's nobody else who's even remotely thin enough to fit into that suit. Carlie's car is stuck in a snowdrift. If you don't play Santa's helper there'll be no one to—"

The ring of the phone stopped Wendy mid-sentence. The next thing Shannon heard was Wendy's happy voice saying, "Raleigh's Department Store. Shannon Raleigh's assistant, Wendy, speaking."

In the lull while Wendy obviously listened to the caller, Shannon cast another critical eye over her reflection. The little red dress was kind of cute. The color complemented her long black hair and made her blue eyes seem bluer. If she were wearing it anywhere else, she'd actually think she looked pretty.

A long-forgotten ache filled her. It was the first time in a year she *felt* pretty, sexy. But sexy wasn't exactly the way a grown woman should dress in a room filled with babies, toddlers and elementary school kids.

The ache was quickly replaced by fear—which was the real reason she didn't want to play Santa's helper. How could she spend four hours in a room full of adorable children? She wanted a baby so badly it hurt, but she couldn't have kids. And seeing all those sweet faces, hearing their cute little lists, would crush her.

"Um, Shannon?"

"I'm not coming out."

"Fine. That was Tammy in the shoe department. No one's come into the store for the past hour and she could tell the storm was getting worse, so she checked the forecast on the internet. They have no clue how much snow we're going to get, but they aren't shy about suggesting we might get another foot."

"Another foot!"

Shannon raced out of her bathroom and pulled back the curtain behind her huge mahogany desk. Thick fluffy snowflakes cascaded from the sky, coating the tinsel and silver bells on the streetlamps of Main Street, Green Hill, Pennsylvania. It blanketed the Christmas lights that outlined shop doorways, and sat on the roof of the park's gazebo like a tall white hat.

"Holy cow!"

Her gaze on the little red Santa's helper outfit, Wendy also said, "Holy cow."

"Don't make fun. We have a serious problem here." Or maybe a way out. She turned from the window. "I think it's time t

on her keyboard, she acti-
ks and the alarm system.
, she peered down at her
utfit. She should change,
ads were getting worse
inute, she simply yanked

I'll call the radio stations so they can add us to their list of closings. Then I'll lock up."

As the announcement went out over the loudspeaker, Shannon called all the local radio stations and advised them to let listeners know Raleigh's would be closed for the night.

Just as she hung up the phone from the final call, Wendy peeked in. "Okay. Fifteen minutes are up. Store's empty."

"Great. Thanks. Be careful going home."

"My boyfriend's coming to pick me up in his truck. I'll be fine."

Shannon smiled. "See you tomorrow."

"If we can make it."

"We better hope we can make it. The weekend before Christmas is our busiest time."

Wendy shrugged. "If shoppers don't get here tomorrow, they'll just come on Sunday or Monday or Tuesday or whatever. Nobody's going to go without gifts this Christmas. I'd say your profits are safe."

Shannon laughed. Wendy waved and headed off. With a few clicks
vated the building lo
Reaching for her coa
little Santa's helper
but knowing the r
with every passing

her long white wool coat from the closet and ran out.

At the end of the hall, she pushed on the swinging door that led from executive row to housewares. Striding to the elevator, she passed shelves and tables bulging with merchandise, all under loops of tinsel and oversized ornaments hanging from the low ceiling. On the first floor, she hurried past the candy department, to the back door and the employee parking lot. Putting her SUV into four-wheel drive, she edged onto the street and slowly wound along the twisty road that took her out into the country, to her home five miles outside the small city.

As she stepped out into the eighteen inches of snow in her driveway, a sense of disconnect shivered through her. Though it had been a year, it felt like only yesterday that she had been married and living in sunny, happy Charleston, South Carolina, where people didn't often see snow, let alone need winter coats and boots. Then she'd been diagnosed with stage-four endometriosis and forced to have a hysterectomy, her husband had unceremoniously divorced her and she'd returned home to the comforting arms of her parents.

But just when she'd gotten adjusted to being back in town and working at the store, her parents had retired and moved to Florida. Worse, they now wanted her to sell the store to fund their retirement.

Once again, she was alone—and soon she'd be unemployed.

She trudged up the back steps to the kitchen door, scolding herself for being so negative. She knew what was wrong. The near miss with playing Santa's helper had rattled her. Four hours of ushering kids to Santa's throne and listening to their sweet voices as they gave their Christmas lists to the jolly old elf would have been her undoing—a bittersweet reminder to her that she'd never bring a child into this world.

Inside the cold yellow kitchen, she'd just barely unwound the scarf from her neck when the doorbell rang. Confused, she walked up the hall, dodging the boxes of Christmas decorations she'd brought from the attic the night before. She flipped on the porch light and yanked open the door.

A snow-covered state policeman took off his hat. "Evening, ma'am. I'm Trooper Potter."

She blinked. What the devil would the police want with her? "Good evening."

Then Trooper Potter shifted a bit to his left and she saw Rory Wallace. All six foot one, no more than one hundred and eighty-five gorgeous pounds of him. His black hair and topcoat were sprinkled with snow. His dark eyes were wary, apologetic.

"Rory?"

"Good evening, Shannon."

The policeman angled his thumb behind him. "I see you know Mr. Wallace."

"Yes. I do." How could she forget a dark-haired, dark-eyed sex god? While he had dated her roommate, Natalie, their first year at university, Shannon had had a secret crush on him. With his high cheekbones, well-defined chin, broad shoulders and flat abs, he had the kind of looks that made women swoon and Shannon wasn't blind.

"Mr. Wallace was stranded on the interstate. The hotels filled up quickly with travelers and now his only options are a cot in the high school gym or finding someone to take him in. He tells me that he's in Pennsylvania because he has business with you on Monday and—"

"I came a few days early to get a look at the store on my own," Rory interrupted, stepping forward. "But I ran into the storm. I was hoping you wouldn't mind me staying the night. Normally, I wouldn't ask such a big favor, but as you can see I'm desperate."

Mind? She almost laughed. She would bet

that fifty percent of the women he met fantasized about being stuck in a storm with him.

She opened the door a little wider. Not only would having him stay the night get her out of the doldrums about her life, but this also had all the makings of a perfect fantasy. Cold night. Gorgeous guy. And wine. She had tons of wine.

"Daddy, I'm cold."

Her fantasy came to an abrupt halt as she glanced down and saw a little girl standing beside Rory. She wore a pink ski jacket and carried a matching pink backpack. Little strands of yellow hair peeked from beneath her hood.

Her heart pinched with fear. Her breathing stuttered out. Did Fate think it was funny to let her dodge playing Santa's helper only to drop an adorable child on her doorstep?

"You can see why I don't want to stay in a shelter."

Fear and yearning collided as she glanced down at the sweet little girl with big blue eyes and fine yellow hair. As much as she knew spending time with this child would intensify her longing for her own children, she couldn't leave Rory and his daughter out in the cold or ship them to a crowded gym with hundreds of other noisy travelers and a tiny cot.

She also couldn't be a Scrooge. Her problem wasn't their problem. She would be a good hostess.

She stepped back so they could enter. "Yes. Yes, of course."

Carrying a duffel bag and briefcase as he squeezed into the foyer, Rory brushed against her, setting off a firestorm of sensations inside her. She ignored them. Not just because a man with a child was most likely married, but because she probably wouldn't have made a pass at him even if he'd been alone. In the year since her divorce, she hadn't been able to relate to men as anything other than employees. After her husband's anger over her inability to have kids and the way he'd dropped her like a hot potato—no consideration for their five-year marriage, no consideration for her devastation—the fear of another man rejecting her paralyzed her.

Plus, come Monday, they'd be doing business. His family owned a holding company for various types of stores and Raleigh's would probably fit their collection. That's why she'd thought of Natalie's old boyfriend when her parents had decided they wanted to sell the store. It could be a quick, painless sale. She didn't want to jeopardize that.

But, wow. It had been fun to fantasize about being stranded with him, fun for the ten seconds before reality intruded, reminding her she wasn't normal.

As Rory dropped his duffel bag, she said, "It's a terrible storm."

"Worst in ten years," the trooper agreed, staying behind on the porch. "If you're all settled, I need to get back on the road."

"We're fine," Shannon said, as she began to close the door. As an afterthought, she added, "Thank you."

"Yes, thank you," Rory Wallace called out, too.

Already on his way down her front steps, the trooper waved goodbye and trudged through the thick snow on the sidewalk to his car.

Awkward silence reigned as Rory Wallace took in the foyer of Shannon Raleigh's home. As if it wasn't bad enough that he'd been forced to humble himself and ask for shelter from a business associate, it appeared she was moving. Boxes blocked half the corridor that led from the foyer to the kitchen behind it. They littered the living room to the right and the dining room to the left.

Which made him feel even guiltier. "Thank you. I really appreciate this."

She smiled graciously. "You're welcome." Then she shivered, even though she wore a long white coat and the house wasn't that cold, just chilled, as if the heat had been on low all day while she was at work. "Give me a minute to turn on the furnace." She walked to a thermostat on the wall and adjusted it. "You might want to keep your coats on until it heats up in here."

He unbuttoned his topcoat. "Actually, after spending ten hours in a car, your house is warm to us." He stooped to help his daughter with her jacket. Realizing he'd never introduced her, he peeked up at Shannon. "This is my daughter, Finley."

Crouching beside them, Shannon said, "It's nice to meet you, Finley."

Finley mumbled, "Nice to meet you, too," then she looked at him as if wanting to make sure he'd noticed that she'd been polite.

Sliding her arms out of her little pink jacket, he gave her a subtle nod of approval. Lately, Finley had been something of a six-year-old diva. Disciplining her worked, but not always. And some days he was at his wits' end with her. So he was lucky she'd been polite to Shannon Raleigh. He didn't know how he'd deal with her if she insulted the woman who'd rescued them.

"This is the perfect night to be stranded with me," Shannon said, taking Finley's jacket to the closet behind her. "My parents will be home from Florida next Saturday and I promised I'd have the house decorated for Christmas. All these boxes are decorations they left behind when they moved to Florida. You can help me."

While Rory breathed a sigh of relief that he hadn't interrupted her moving, Finley's nose wrinkled and her eyes narrowed with distaste. Before he realized what she was about to do, she spat, "I hate Christmas."

Shannon reared back as if someone had slapped her. Her pretty blue eyes widened in disbelief. "Hate Christmas? How can you hate Christmas?"

"How can you believe that a fat guy in a red suit brings you presents?"

Anger pulsed through Rory's veins and he shot Finley a warning look. He wouldn't yell at her in front of Shannon, but he did need to provide a few rules for behavior when imposing on someone they barely knew. He faced Shannon. "Why don't you tell me where we're sleeping and I'll take Finley to our room and help her get settled in."

Shannon winced. "Actually, there's only one bedroom."

"Oh."

"It's no big deal. We'll give the bed to Finley, and you and I will use sleeping bags. You can put yours on the floor beside the bed and I'll sleep on the sofa."

Mortal embarrassment overwhelmed him. He hadn't realized how much he'd be putting her out when he gave her name to the state policeman. "This is such an imposition. You can't give us your room. Finley and I don't mind sleeping in the living room."

Finley stomped her foot. "I don't want to sleep on the floor."

He flashed Finley another warning look. "You won't. You can have the sofa."

"I want a bed!"

Rory's head pounded. He understood that this time of year wasn't easy for Finley. Her mom had left on Christmas day two years before. So every year, she got moody, and every year he indulged her by taking her on vacation from Christmas Eve to New Year's. For a guy who'd also lost his marriage on Christmas day, a vacation from the holiday was good for him, too. But the foot-stomping and the pouting and the demands that everything go her way, those had just started. And he absolutely refused to get on board with them. He had to spend the next week looking at Raleigh's Department Store for his family's holding company. He couldn't have her acting like a brat all week.

He turned to Shannon. "Would you mind showing us to the bedroom so I can get Finley settled?"

"Not at all."

She led them into a small first-floor bedroom that was as neat and clean as the rest of the house…minus boxes. A feminine white ruffled spread sat on a simple double bed. Red pillows on the bed matched the red shag carpet beneath it and the drapes on the double windows.

He dropped his duffel bag to the floor. "Wow."

She faced him with a smile. Her shiny black hair was a wonderland of long, springy curls. In the years since university, her face had shifted just slightly and she'd become a softer, prettier version of the young girl he remembered.

"Wow?"

"I'm just a little surprised by your room."

Her smile grew. "Really? Why?"

"The red." He felt the same color rising on his cheeks. The room was girlie, yet incredibly sexy. But he certainly didn't feel comfortable saying that to the woman giving him and his daughter shelter, especially not after Finley's minitantrum. Still, he never would have guessed this sexy combination of color and style from the sweet Shannon he knew all those years ago at school.

"There's a private bathroom for the bedroom—" she gestured toward a door to the right "—over there."

"Thank you."

"Just come out when you're ready." She smiled. "I'll start supper. I hope you like toasted cheese sandwiches and soup. I'm not much of a cook."

"On a cold day like this, soup is terrific."

She closed the door behind her and Rory crouched down in front of Finley. Smoothing his hand down her shiny yellow hair, he said, "You're killing me."

She blinked innocently "What?"

"Ms. Raleigh is doing us a favor by letting us stay. We should be polite to her."

"I was polite."

"Saying you want the bed while you stomp your foot is not polite."

Her bottom lip puffed out. "Sorry."

And *this* was why he had trouble disciplining her. The second he pointed out something she'd done wrong, she turned on that little-girl charm. Batted her long black lashes over her pretty blue eyes.

Scrubbing his hand over his mouth, he rose.

"I'll tell you what. You stay in here for a few minutes, while I spend some time getting acquainted with our hostess." And apologizing and doing damage control. "While I'm gone, you can get your pajamas and toothbrush out of your backpack and think about how you'd want a little girl to behave if she were a guest in our house."

Apparently liking her assignment, she nodded eagerly.

"And don't spend all your time thinking about how you'd spoil your little guest, because you wouldn't. If you had to give up your bed for a stranger, you'd want her to be nice to you."

Finley nodded again and said, "Okay. I get it."

Rory was absolutely positive she didn't, but he had to make amends to Shannon. He left Finley in the bedroom and walked up the hall to the kitchen.

The house was small, but comfortable. The furniture was new and expensive, an indication that Raleigh's Department Store did, indeed, make lots of money. So maybe the trip to Pennsylvania might not have been the mistake he'd thought while sitting in his car for ten hours, not moving, on the interstate?

He found Shannon in the kitchen. Still wearing her coat, she drew bread from a drawer and cheese from the refrigerator.

"Thanks again for taking us in."

"No problem." She set the bread and cheese on the center island of the sunny yellow kitchen with light oak cabinets and pale brown granite countertops. She reached for the top button of her coat. "Furnace has kicked in," she said with a laugh, popping the first button and the second, but when she reached for the third, she paused. "I think I'll just take this out to the hall closet."

She walked past him, to the swinging door. Wanting something to do, he followed her. Just as he said, "Is there anything I can do to help with supper?" her coat fell off her shoulders, revealing a bright red dress.

But when she turned in surprise, he saw the dress wasn't really a dress but some little red velvet thing that dipped low at the bodice, revealing an enticing band of cleavage. Tall black boots showcased her great legs.

She was dressed like Mrs. Santa—if Mrs. Santa were a young, incredibly endowed woman who liked short skirts.

His dormant hormones woke as if from a long winter's nap, and he took a step back. These little bursts of attraction he was having toward her were all wrong. He had an unruly daughter who took priority over everything in his life, including his hormones, and he was a guest in Shannon's house. Plus, tomorrow morning, when the storm was over, they'd go into her department store as adversaries of a sort. She'd be trying to sell her family business to him and he'd be looking for reasons not to buy. He couldn't be attracted to her.

He swallowed back the whole filing cabinet of flirtatious remarks that wanted to come out. "That's an interesting choice of work clothes."

She laughed nervously. "I was going to fill in for our Santa's helper in the toy department."

Ah. Not Mrs. Santa but Santa's helper.

"Well, the dress is very…" He paused. He knew the dress was probably supposed to be Christmassy and cute. And on a shorter woman it probably was. But she was tall, sleek, yet somehow still womanly. He didn't dare tell her that. "Festive."

She brought the coat to her neck, using it to shield herself. "That's the look we're after. Festive and happy. And it actually works for the girl who fits into this costume. I was lucky Mother Nature saved me and I didn't have to fill in for her tonight."

Recognizing her acute nervousness, Rory pulled his gaze away from her long, slim legs.

He cleared his throat. "I…um…just followed you to see if I could help you with anything."

She motioned toward his black suit and white shirt. "Are you sure you want to butter bread or stir tomato soup in a suit?"

He took off his jacket, loosened his tie and began rolling up his sleeves.

And Shannon's mouth watered. Damn it. She'd already figured out she couldn't be fantasizing about him. Sure, his shoulders were broad, his arms muscled. And she'd always been a sucker for a man in a white shirt with rolled-up sleeves looking like he was ready to get down to business. But as far as she could tell, he was married. That shut down the possibility of any relationship right then and there. Plus, she wanted him to buy her parents' store. She couldn't be drooling on him.

She hung up her coat, then scurried past him, into the kitchen and directly to the laundry room. Leaning on the closed door, she drew in a deep breath. God, he was gorgeous. But he was also married.

Married. Married. Married.

She forced the litany through her head, hoping it would sink in, as she grabbed a pair of sweats and a T-shirt from the dryer and changed into them.

When she returned to the kitchen he stood at the center island, buttering bread. "While we have a few seconds of privacy, I also wanted to apologize for Finley. I brought her because she's on Christmas break from school and I hate to leave her with her nanny for an entire week. But I know she can be a handful."

Walking over to join him, she said, "She's just a little girl."

"True, but she's also recently entered a new phase of some sort where she stomps her foot when she doesn't get her own way."

Standing so close to him, she could smell his aftershave. Her breathing stuttered in and out of her lungs. So she laughed, trying to cover it. "A new phase, huh?"

"She was perfectly fine in preschool and kindergarten, but first grade is turning her into a diva."

"Diva?"

"Yeah." Smiling, he caught her gaze, and every nerve ending in her body lit up like the lights on the Christmas tree in Central Park. Spinning away from him, she repeated the litany in her head again.

Married. Married. Married!

"You know, I can easily handle this myself.

You can use the den for privacy if you need to call your wife."

He snorted a laugh. "Not hardly."

She set the frying pan for the sandwiches on the stove and faced him again. "I'm sure she's worried."

"And I'm sure she and her new husband aren't even thinking about me and Finley right now."

"Oh." Nerves rolled through her. He was divorced? Not married?

Their gazes caught. Attraction spun through her like snowflakes dancing in the light of a streetlamp. She reminded herself that they were about to do business, but it didn't work to snuff out the snap and crackle of electricity sizzling between them.

She pivoted away from him. Pretending she needed all her concentration to open two cans of soup, she managed to avoid conversation. But that didn't stop the chatter in her brain. As difficult as it might be to have a little girl around, she was abundantly glad Finley was with him. She might have had that quick fantasy of being stranded with him, but now that sanity had returned, she knew the sale of the store had to take precedence over a night of…she swallowed…passion? Good God, she hadn't even *thought* the word in a year, let alone *experienced* it. She'd probably dissolve into a puddle if he made a pass at her.

Finley came out of the bedroom just as Rory set the sandwiches on the table and Shannon had finished ladling soup into the bright green bowls sitting on the pretty yellow place mats. She crawled onto a chair and spread her paper napkin on her lap.

Longing hit Shannon like an unexpected burst of winter wind. She remembered dreams of buying pretty dresses for her own little girl, her dreams of taking her to the park, gymnastics, dance lessons and soccer—

She stopped her thoughts, cut off the sadness and grief that wanted to engulf her. Surely, she could have a little girl in her house without breaking into a million shattered pieces? She hadn't given up on the idea of becoming a mother altogether. She knew that once she adjusted to not having her own child, she could adopt. So maybe this was a good time to begin adjusting?

Finley sighed. "I don't like red soup."

Sounding very parental, Rory said, "That's okay. Just eat your sandwich."

Finley sighed heavily again, as if it were pure torture not to get her own way. Rory ignored her. Shannon studied her curiously, realizing that with Diva Finley she really would get a solid understanding of what it took to be a parent. She was like a little blond-haired litmus test for whether or not Shannon had what it took to adopt a child and be a mom.

Rory turned to her and said, "This is certainly a lovely old house."

She faced Rory so quickly that their gazes collided. He had the darkest eyes she'd ever seen. And they were bottomless. Mesmerizing…

She gave herself a mental shake. It was pointless to be attracted. He wouldn't make a pass at her with his daughter around, and she wouldn't make a pass at him because they were about to do business. She had to stop noticing these things.

She cleared her throat. "The parts I've restored are great. But the whole heating system needs to be replaced."

"Well, you've done a wonderful job on the renovations you have done."

"Really?" She peeked up at him.

And everything Rory wanted to say fell out of his head. Her big blue eyes reminded him of the sky in summer. The black curls that curved around her face had his hand itching to touch them.

Finley sighed heavily. "I don't want this soup."

Rory faced her. "We already agreed that you didn't have to eat it."

"I don't like that it's here."

"Here?"

"In front of me!"

Before Rory had a chance to react, Shannon rose with a smile. "Let me take it to the sink."

She reached across the table, lifted the bowl and calmly walked it to the sink. Then she returned to the table and sat as if nothing had happened.

Technically nothing *had* happened. She'd diffused the potentially problematic soup episode just by reacting calmly.

Of course, he knew that was what *he* should have done, but after ten grueling hours on the road, he was every bit as tired and cranky as Finley. And this confusing attraction he felt for Shannon wasn't helping things.

"I don't want this sandwich."

Here we go again. "Finley—"

"I'm tired."

Before Rory could remind her he was, too, Shannon rose. "I have just the cure for being tired. A bubble bath."

Finley instantly brightened. "Really?"

"I have all kinds of bubbles in my bathroom.

It's right beside the bedroom you're using. Why don't we go get a bath ready for you?"

Finley all but bounced off her chair. "All right!"

They disappeared down the hall to the bedroom, and Rory ran his hand down his face.

He didn't know what would drive him crazy first, his daughter or his hormones.

CHAPTER TWO

SHANNON WALKED OUT of the kitchen with a happy Finley skipping behind her to the bathroom. Her self-pity long forgotten and her new mission in place, she was glad to help tired, frazzled Rory with his daughter. It would give her a chance for some one-on-one time with Finley, a chance to prove to herself that she was strong enough to be around kids. Strong enough to adopt one of her own, if she wanted to.

Unfortunately, the second they were out of Rory's earshot, Finley the Diva returned. "You can go. I'll fill the tub myself."

Having watched her friends in Charleston handle their children, if nothing else, Shannon knew the grown-up in charge had to stay in charge. "I'm sure you could, but I want to do it."

Finley crossed her arms on her chest and huffed out a sigh.

For Rory's sake, Shannon didn't laugh. "I like this scent," she said, picking up her favorite bubble bath. "But you can choose whichever one you want."

Finley chose another scent. Shannon shrugged. It didn't matter to her which scent Finley used. She turned on the tap, poured in the liquid and faced Finley with a smile. "I'm going to leave the room while this fills up so you can undress. Call me when you're ready to step in the tub."

"I don't need help."

And with that comment, Shannon decided she had experimented enough for one night. She didn't have the right to discipline this little girl and she definitely needed a firm hand. So she left this battle for Rory. "Okay. That's great."

She walked out of the bathroom and directly into the kitchen. "Tub is almost full and Finley's stripping. You might want to go in and supervise."

Rory rose. "She can bathe herself but I like to be in the next room just in case." He glanced at the dishes and winced. "Sorry about that."

She waved a hand in dismissal. "I can load a few dishes into the dishwasher. You go on ahead."

Alone in the kitchen for forty minutes, she

wasn't sure if Finley had decided to have an Olympic swim in her tub or if Rory was reading her a story…or if they'd found the TV and decided to stay on their own in the bedroom.

Whatever had happened, Shannon was fine with it. She knew they were both tired, weary. And once the dishes were stacked in the dishwasher and the kitchen cleaned, she had decorating to do. But just as she dragged the box of garland over to the sofa, Rory walked into the living room.

"Well, she's down for the night."

"I suspected she was tired."

"Exhausted."

"She'll be happy in the morning."

With a weary sigh, Rory fell to the couch. "How'd you get so smart about kids?"

His praise surprised her. Though she'd spent years watching her friends' kids, longing for her own, she'd also all but ignored them this past difficult year. "I had some friends in South Carolina who had children. I used to babysit."

He laughed. "You *volunteered* to hang around kids?"

"It's always easier to handle children who aren't yours." She brushed her hands together to rid them of attic dust and stepped away from the box of decorations. Eager to change the subject, she said, "You sound like you could use a glass of wine."

"Or a beer, if you have one."

"I do." She left the living room, got two beers from the refrigerator and gave one to Rory.

He relaxed on the couch, closed his eyes. "Thanks."

"You're welcome." She glanced at the decorations, thinking she really should get started, but also knowing Rory was embarrassed about imposing and at his wits' end. Deciding to be a Good Samaritan and give him someone to talk to, she gingerly sat on the sofa beside him. "Must have been some drive."

"There was a point when I considered turning around because I could see things were getting worse, but the weather reports kept saying the storm would blow out soon." He peered over at her. "It never did."

"This will teach you to listen to weathermen."

He laughed. Relaxed a little more. "So you ended up taking over your family's business?"

"By default. I was perfectly happy to work with the buyers and in advertising for Raleigh's. But my dad wanted to retire and I'm an only child." She paused then smiled at him. "I see you also ended up in your dad's job."

Rory tilted his head, studying her. Her smile

was pretty, genuine. Not flirtatious and certainly not enough to get his hormones going, but an odd tingle took up residence in his stomach. "Yeah. I did. Who would have thought ten years ago that we'd be running the two businesses we always talked about while I waited for Natalie for our dates?"

"Well, you were a shoo-in for your job. You're the oldest son of a family that owns a business. I thought I was going to be a lawyer. Turns out law school is really, really dull."

He laughed again, then realized he couldn't remember the last time he'd laughed twice, back-to-back, in the same night. Warmth curled through him. Not like arousal from flirting. Not like happiness, but something else. Something richer. Not only was Shannon Raleigh a knockout and good with kids, but she was also easy to talk to—

Good grief. This strange feeling he was having was attraction. Real attraction. The next step beyond the hormone-driven reaction he had when he saw her in the little red dress.

Damn it. He was here to look at her family's store to see if it was an appropriate investment for his family. He couldn't be attracted to her. Not just that, but he was already a loser at love. He'd given in to the fun of flirting once. He'd let himself become vulnerable. Hell, he'd let himself tumble head over heels for someone, and he knew how that had turned out—with her leaving him on Christmas day two years ago, and all but deserting their daughter.

When he'd finally found her and asked about visitation, she'd told him she didn't want to see Finley. Ever. Hoping that she'd change her mind in the two years that had passed, he'd run out of excuses to give Finley for missed birthdays and holidays. Pretty soon he was going to have to tell a six-year-old girl that her mother didn't want her.

That broke his heart. Shattered it into a million painful pieces. Made him want to shake his ex-wife silly.

Which was why he'd never marry again. At this point in his life he wasn't even sure he'd date again.

He rose from the sofa. "You know what? I'm tired, too. I'm going to have to figure out how to get my car from the interstate in the morning and I'm guessing for that I'm going to need a good night's sleep." He gave her a warm smile. "Thanks again for letting us stay."

With that he turned and all but raced toward the door, but he didn't get three steps before Shannon stopped him. "Rory?"

He turned.

She pointed at the sleeping bag rolled up at by the door. “You might want to take that.”

He sucked in a breath. The whole point of coming into the room had been to get his sleeping bag. Two minutes in her company and he’d forgotten that. “Yeah. Thanks.”

He scooped the sleeping bag from the floor. He hadn’t been this foolish around a woman in years.

He was glad he was leaving in the morning.

Shannon was awakened by the feeling of soft breath puffing in her face. She batted at it only to have her hand meet something solid.

Finley yelled, “Ouch!”

Shannon bolted up on the couch as several things popped into her head at once. First, she was sleeping in her living room. Second, she had company. Third, Finley was not the nicest child in the world. But, the all-important fourth, she would be alone with a child until Rory woke up.

“I’m hungry.” Finley’s tiny face scrunched. Her nose became a wrinkled button. Her mouth pulled down in an upside-down *U*.

Shannon pressed her lips together to keep from laughing. Which heartened her. Because

Finley was forceful and demanding, not a cute little cuddle bug, it was easier for Shannon to deal with being around her.

She rolled out of her sleeping bag. Her friends had complained about being awakened by their children at ungodly hours. But a glance at the wall clock told her it was after eight. She couldn't fault Finley for waking her. It might be Saturday, but she still had to be at the store by ten to open it.

Fortunately, she had enough time to make something to eat. "Well, I enjoy cooking breakfast so it looks like we're both lucky this morning."

That confused Finley so much that her frown wobbled.

Laughing, Shannon ruffled her hair. "Which do you prefer pancakes or waffles?"

"Do you have blueberries?"

"Of course."

"Then I'd like pancakes."

Shannon headed for the kitchen. "You and I are going to get along very well."

As she pulled the ingredients for pancakes from the cupboards, Finley took a seat at the table. Before she started to make the batter, Shannon picked up the remote for her stereo and turned it on. A rousing rendition of "Here Comes Santa Claus" poured into the room.

"Would you like a glass of milk?"

"Yes, please."

Shannon dipped into her refrigerator as Finley slid off her seat. Watching Finley walk to the counter, she grabbed the gallon of milk and pulled it out of the fridge. But before she could reach the counter, Finley had picked up the remote and turned off the music.

She blinked. "I was listening to that."

"It was stupid."

"It was a Christmas song."

"And Christmas is stupid."

Shannon gaped at her. Not just because she had the audacity to turn off the music without asking, but that was the second time she'd mentioned she didn't like Christmas.

The temptation was strong to ask why, as she poured Finley a glass of milk, but she wasn't quite sure how to approach it. Did she say, *Hey, kid, everybody likes Christmas. You get gifts. You get cookies. What's the deal?*

As curious as she was, that seemed a lot like interfering and she was just getting accustomed to being around a child. She wasn't ready for deep, personal interaction yet. Plus, saying she hated Christmas could just be a part of one of

Finley the Diva's tantrums. Or a way to manipulate people.

So, she turned to the counter and began preparing pancakes. A happy hum started in her throat and worked its way out, surprising her. Breakfast was one of the few meals she was well versed in. She could make a pancake or a waffle with the best of them. But it was a happy surprise to be able to be in the same room with Finley without worrying that she'd fall apart or dwell on her inability to have kids herself.

"So where do you go to school?"

"Winchester Academy."

"Is that a private school?"

Finley nodded.

"Do you like school?"

"Sometimes. Artie Regan brings frogs and scares me. And Jenny Logan beats me to the swing."

A motherly warmth flowed through her. When she wasn't demanding her own way, Finley was normal. And here she was handling her. Talking to her. No flutters of panic. No feeling sorry for herself.

The kitchen door opened and Rory walked into the room yawning. "Sorry about that."

"About what?" Shannon faced him with a

smile, but the smile disappeared as her mouth went dry.

His dark hair was sticking out in all directions. His eyes didn't seem to want to open. A day-old growth of beard sexily shadowed his chin and cheeks. He wore a white undershirt and navy blue sweats that loosely clung to his lean hips.

"About sleeping in. Normally, I'm up—" He paused. "Are you making pancakes?"

"Blueberry."

"Wow. We should get stranded on an interstate more often."

She laughed. *Laughed.* She had a sexy man and a cute little girl in her kitchen and she wasn't stuttering or shattering, she was laughing.

But a little warning tweaked her brain. Not only was she enjoying this way too much, but it also would be over soon. They'd eat breakfast, pack up the few things they'd brought with them and head out.

She had about twenty minutes over breakfast before she'd be alone again.

Rory ambled to the counter, where the coffeemaker sputtered the last drops of fresh coffee into the pot. "Can I get you a cup?"

"That'd be great, thanks. Mugs are in the cupboard by the sink."

But as he reached into the cupboard to get the mugs, his arm stopped. "Holy cats!"

Shannon paused her spoon in the pancake batter. "What?"

"There's got to be two feet of snow out there."

"That was the eventual predication after we already had eighteen inches."

"Yeah, well, it doesn't look like the snowplow went through."

She dropped the spoon, hustled to the window beside him. "Wow."

He turned and caught her gaze. "Even with that big SUV I saw in the driveway, I'll bet you can't get us out to a main road."

Her heart lodged in her throat. Could they actually be forced to stay another day? Could she handle another day?

The answer came swiftly, without hesitation. She couldn't just handle another day; she *wanted* another day.

"With all that snow, I'm not sure the main roads are even clear."

"I'll check the internet."

"If the roads are still closed, you know you're welcome to stay, right?"

"I think we may have to take you up on that."

Though her heart leaped with anticipation, she pasted a disappointed-for-them look on her face. “I’m sorry.”

“I’m the one who’s sorry.”

“Don’t be.” She brightened her expression. “I don’t mind.”

Rory nudged his head toward Finley, who sat quietly at the kitchen table.

Lowering her voice, Shannon said, “She’ll be fine.”

“You want to be the one to tell her?”

“What do you say we get a pancake into her first?”

He tapped her nose. “Excellent idea.”

The friendly tap shouldn’t have made Shannon’s heart race, but it did. She pivoted away from him and returned to her pancake batter. They were staying another day as guests. Friends. Nothing more. But being friends meant no stress. No pressure. They could have a good time.

A good time, instead of a lonely, boring weekend.

Who would have thought the day before, when she’d stood trembling with fear over playing Santa’s helper, that today she’d welcome having a little girl spend the day with her?

She ladled batter onto the already warm grill

and within minutes the sweet scent of pancakes filled the air.

As she piled pancakes on three plates, Rory found the maple syrup and took the pot of coffee to the table.

Finley eagerly grabbed her plate from Shannon. Without as much as a blink from her dad, she said, "Thank you."

Shannon's heart tweaked again. She glanced from happy Finley to relieved Rory. They had no idea how much their presence meant to her. Worse, they probably didn't realize she was actually glad the snowplow hadn't yet gone through. Their misery changed her incredibly lonely, probably bordering-toward-pathetic weekend into time with other people. Company for dinner the night before. Someone to make pancakes for. People who would eat lunch and maybe dinner with her.

And maybe even someone to bake sugar cookies with? A little girl who'd paint them with her child's hand, giving them strokes and color and even mistakes only a child could make. Turning them into real Christmas cookies.

Rory pointed at his pancake. "These are great."

Finley nodded in agreement. "These are great."

"Thanks."

Rory laughed and caught her gaze. "Thought you said you couldn't cook?"

Her heart stuttered a bit. Not because he was paying attention to her, but because his dark eyes were filled with warmth and happiness. Casual happiness. The kind of happiness real friends shared. "I can't, except for breakfast. But breakfast foods are usually easy."

Turning his attention back to his plate, he said, "Well, these are delicious."

Warmth filled her. Contentment. She gave herself a moment to soak it all in before she reached for her fork and tasted her own pancake.

Picking up his coffee cup, Rory said, "I can't believe how much snow fell."

"It is Pennsylvania."

"How do you deal with it?"

"Well, on days like this, those of us who can stay in."

"You play games maybe?"

Ah, she got what he was doing. He was paving the way to tell Finley they couldn't leave. Probably hoping to show her she'd have a good day if they stayed.

"We do. We play lots of games. But we also bake cookies."

Finley didn't even glance up. Happily involved in her blueberry pancake, she ignored them.

Rory said, "I love cookies."

"These are special cookies. They're sugar cookies that I cut into shapes and then paint."

"Paint?"

"With icing. I put colored icing on houses, churches, bells—"

Finley glanced up sharply. "You mean Christmas bells."

Shannon winced. "Well, yes. I'm baking cookies for my family when we celebrate Christmas next week. But it's still fun—"

"I hate Christmas!"

This was the third time Finley had said she hated Christmas. It wasn't merely part of a tantrum or even a way to manipulate people. This little girl really didn't like Christmas.

"Okay. So instead of baking cookies, how about if we play cards?"

"I thought we were leaving."

Rory set his hand on top of Finley's. "I'd like to leave. But I have to check to see if the roads are open. There's a good possibility that we're stranded here for another few hours, maybe even another day."

Finley sighed heavily, like a billion-dollar heiress who'd just received bad news, and who would, at any second, explode. Shannon found herself holding her breath, waiting for Finley's reply. Which was ridiculous. The kid was six. The weather wasn't anybody's fault. She was stuck and that was that.

Setting her fork on her plate, Shannon rose and said, "While I go to my room to check on the roads and call my staff, you drink your milk and finish your breakfast. Then we'll put the dishes in the dishwasher and we'll play Go Fish."

Finley's eyes narrowed and her mouth formed the upside-down *U* again. But Shannon ignored her. From her peripheral vision she watched Finley glare at her dad.

Without looking at her, Rory said, "I haven't played Go Fish in years. I'm not sure I remember the rules."

"It's an easy game, Daddy."

"Good. Then I should catch on quickly."

Shannon took her plate to the sink. "Or maybe she'll beat you."

That brought a light to Finley's eyes. When Shannon returned from checking the road conditions on the internet, calling her staff to say she wasn't opening the store and calling the radio stations to alert the community that the store would be closed again, she returned to the kitchen. Finley eagerly helped clear the table, stacked dishes in the dishwasher and rifled through a kitchen drawer for a deck of cards.

"I had to close the store."

Rory held up his cell phone. "I figured. I checked the road conditions. Nothing's really open. Customers can't get there anyway."

As Finley approached the table with the cards, Shannon said, "So we'll have some fun."

Pulling a chair away from the round kitchen table, Rory said, "Yes, we will. Right, Finley?"

Finley sighed and shrugged, but also pulled out a chair and sat.

Shannon noticed that Rory more or less let Finley win the first game, so she went along, too. But when Rory handily won the second game, Shannon didn't think it was out of line to play the third game without deference to Finley. But when she won, Finley exploded.

"You cheated!"

Shannon laughed. "No. Cheating takes all the sport out of a game. There's no fun in winning if you haven't really won."

"I don't care!" She swung her arm across the table, sending cards flying. But before her hand could slow down, she also thwacked her milk. The glass went airborne and landed on the floor. Sticky white milk poured everywhere.

Mortally embarrassed by Finley's outburst, Rory bounced from the table. "Finley!"

Finley bounced off her chair and raced to the kitchen door. "I hate you!"

The swinging door slammed closed when she flew through it.

Shannon rose and grabbed the paper towels. "Sorry. I should have let her win again."

Rory rubbed his hand across the back of his neck. "No. We were playing a game. She knows she can't win every time." He rubbed his neck again. He'd only ever told his parents about the trouble in his marriage and he certainly hadn't intended to tell Shannon because, technically, they didn't really know each other. But deep down Finley was a sweet little girl who deserved defending.

He fell to his seat again. "Finley's behavior isn't the fault of a confused six-year-old, but a mom who abandoned her."

Using a paper towel to sop up the milk, Shannon said, "What?"

"Her mom," Rory said, not quite sure how to broach this subject because he hadn't spoken with anyone about his ex. So he had no practice, no frame of reference for what to say.

He lifted his eyes until he could catch Shannon's gaze. "Finley's mom left us two years ago on Christmas day."

Shannon took the wet paper towels to the trash. Confusion laced her voice when she said, "Your ex left you on Christmas day?"

"Yeah, that's why Finley's sensitive about Christmas. But what's worse is that her mom doesn't want to see her at all. She doesn't like kids. Didn't want kids."

Shannon returned to the table and fell to her chair, trying to force all that to sink in but not quite able to comprehend. She'd spent her entire adult life attempting to get pregnant, longing for a child, and Finley's mom had left her without a backward glance?

"My ex never did anything she didn't want to do." He rose from the chair, pushed it out of his way and stooped to pick up the scattered cards.

"That's amazing."

He shrugged, but his pinched expression told her he wasn't so cavalier about it. "She'd said at the outset of our marriage that she didn't want kids." Finished gathering the cards, he rose. "Her getting pregnant was a surprise, but I thought we were ready. Turns out she wasn't."

Shannon sat in stunned silence. Rory's wife had *abandoned* her daughter? Disbelief thundered through her, along with a sense of injustice. While she'd do anything, give anything, to be able to have a child, Finley's mom had simply abandoned one?

How could a woman be so cruel?

CHAPTER THREE

RORY NEATLY STACKED the cards on the table. "I need to check on her."

"Okay. I'll start lunch."

As she had the night before, Shannon made soup and sandwiches. This time, she chose chicken soup—a soup with not even a red vegetable in it—and prepared a plate of cold cuts and some bread.

Finley walked into the kitchen in front of her dad, who had both hands on her little shoulders. Looking at the floor, she mumbled, "I'm sorry."

Shannon's heart ached for her, but she didn't think it was appropriate to say, "Hey, it's not your fault. Your mom's a horrible woman who shouldn't have left you." So, instead, she said, "That's okay. I didn't make red soup today."

Finley peeked at her. "You didn't?"

"No. I made chicken noodle."

"I like chicken noodle."

"So do I."

Rory got bowls from the cupboard and he and Finley set them on the place mats Shannon had already put out. Finley found soup spoons. Shannon set the cold cuts on the table. Everybody did everything without saying a word.

Shannon felt oddly responsible. Should she have tried to lose at the card game? Should she have reacted differently to the cheating accusation? She honestly didn't know. But she did know Finley deserved a bit of happiness and if she could, she intended to provide it.

She sucked in a breath. "You know…I still have a few sleds from when my dad and I used to slide down Parker's Hill when I was a little girl."

Finley's face instantly brightened. "Really?"

"There's a bit of a hill behind this house. I never tried it out for sledding because I just moved here last year, but I'm guessing there might be a place we could sled-ride."

This time Rory said, "Really?"

"Sure. It would be fun. Even if we can't go sledding, getting outside for some fresh air would do us all good."

Rory inclined his head. "Maybe." He faced his daughter. "What do you think?"

"I'd like to sled-ride."

"And we will if we can," Shannon quickly assured her. "As I said, I've never checked out that hill."

"I don't have snow pants."

"You can wear two pair of jeans," Rory suggested.

"And we'll put them in the dryer as soon as we come inside, so they'll be good for tomorrow morning."

The mood clearing the lunch dishes improved significantly from the mood when setting out those same dishes. Finley hurriedly dressed in the multiple jeans and double sweaters. Shannon found a pair of mittens to put over Finley's tiny multicolored striped gloves.

When Finley was ready, Shannon quickly dressed in a pair of jeans and two sweaters. She put her dad's old parka over herself and used insulated gloves for her hands.

They stepped outside onto the back porch and the glare off the snow almost blinded them.

"Wow. It's beautiful."

Shannon glanced around proudly at the snow-covered fir trees that surrounded her little home. "Yes. It is. I loved living in South Carolina—close to the beach," she added, slanting a look at Rory. "But this is home. As annoying as snow is, it is also beautiful."

They trudged from the house to the shed behind the garage and found an old sled and two red saucer sleds. Shannon and Finley took the saucers and Rory hoisted the bigger runner sled off its hook and followed them out, into the bright sunshine again.

Again they trudged through the snow, walking the twenty or thirty feet from the outbuilding to the dip behind the house.

"There are trees."

Shannon glanced at Rory. "I know. That's why I couldn't say for sure we could sled. Without a wide path between the trees, there'd be too much chance we'd hit one and somebody could be hurt."

He walked fifty feet to the left. "Too many trees this way." Then fifty feet to the right. "I found something!" he called, motioning for Shannon and Finley to come over. "There's a perfect space right here."

The "hill" was more of a slope. It eased down nicely for about thirty feet. A wide ledge would stop them before they reached what looked to be a bigger hill. Still, given that Finley was only six, Shannon didn't think they should try to go beyond the ledge.

She tossed her saucer to the snow. "I'm ready."

Finley followed suit. "I'm ready, too."

They plopped onto their saucers, scooted a bit to get them going then careened down the hill. Finley's squealing giggles filled the quiet air. Hearing her, Shannon laughed. They flew down the slope and, as predicted, their saucers ran out of steam on the ledge.

Finley bounced up. "Let's go again!" She grabbed her saucer and started up the hill.

"Walk along the side!" Shannon called. "We don't want to make our slope bumpy from footprints."

To Shannon's complete amazement, Finley said, "Okay!" and moved to the side of the hill.

When they reached the top, Rory said, "Okay, everybody out of my way. I'm taking this puppy for a ride."

He threw the runner sled onto the snow and landed on top of it, sending it racing down the hill. He hit the ledge, but his sled didn't stop. The ledge didn't even slow the sleek runners. Smooth and thin, they whizzed across the ledge as if it were nothing. In seconds Rory and his sled headed down the bigger hill and disappeared.

Finley screamed.

Thinking she was terrified, Shannon spun to face her, but the little girl's face glowed with laughter. Shannon's lips twitched. Then she burst out laughing, too.

"Do you think we'll ever see him again?"

Finley's giggles multiplied. "How far down does the hill go?"

"I don't know. I've never been back that far."

The world around them grew silent. Now that the fun of seeing him disappear was over, Shannon's tummy tugged with concern. As fast as he was going, he could have hit a tree. He could be at the bottom of the hill, unconscious.

"We better go check on him."

"Can we ride our sleds down to the ledge?"

Shannon laughed and patted Finley's head. Kids really had no comprehension of danger. But before she could reply, Rory called, "I'm okay!"

His voice echoed in the silence around them. But knowing he was fine, Shannon tossed her saucer to the ground. "Race you to the ledge."

Finley positioned her sled and jumped on. They squealed with laughter as they sped down the hill. On the ledge, both popped off their sleds, ran to the edge and peered over. At least fifty feet below, Rory dragged his sled up the hill.

He waved.

Finley waved. "Hi, Daddy!" Then she glanced

around when her voice echoed around her. "That is so cool."

"It's a cool place." She turned Finley toward the top of the hill again. "I'll bet we can sled down twice before your dad gets to the ledge."

Finley grabbed her sled. "Okay!"

They raced down another two times before Rory finally joined them on the ledge. "That was some ride."

Shannon peered over the edge. A reasonably wide strip wound between the rows of trees, but the hill itself was steep and long. "I'll bet it was."

He offered the runner sled to her. "Wanna try?"

She laughed. "Not a chance."

"Hey, sledding was your idea. I thought you were a pro."

"I haven't really gone sledding in years—"

Before she could finish her sentence Rory tossed the sled to the ground and punched into her like a linebacker. She fell on the sled. He fell on top of her and they took off down the hill. For several seconds she had no breath. When she finally caught a gulp of air, she screamed. Really screamed. But soon her screams of fear became screams of delight. The thrill of the speed whooshed through her. The wind whipping across her face felt glorious.

They hit the bottom with a thump.

Obviously paying attention to the grove of trees ahead of them, Rory banked left, toppling the sled to a stop. She rolled on the ground. He rolled beside her.

She turned her head to face him; he turned to face her and they burst out laughing.

Finley's little voice echoed down the hill. "Me next, Daddy!"

He bounced up and held his hand out to Shannon, helping her up.

"That was amazing."

He picked up the sled. "I know. It was like being a kid again. Fun. Free." Holding the sled with one hand, he looped his other arm across her shoulders. "Now we have to trudge about fifty feet up a hill."

She laughed, but her insides tickled. Even working at the store, she'd been nothing but lonely in the past year. Not because she didn't have friends. She did. Lots of them. Not because she missed her husband. Any man who'd desert a woman the day she had a hysterectomy was an ass. But because she'd missed belonging. With Rory and Finley she felt as if she belonged.

She sucked in a breath, erasing that thought.

These two would be with her for one more day—well, one evening and one night. Maybe breakfast in the morning. She couldn't get attached to them.

Still, when they reached the top and found Finley bouncing with delight, happiness filled her again. Finley was a sweet little girl who deserved some fun. Maybe even a break from the reality of her life—that her mom didn't want her.

Rory scooped her off the ground and fell with her onto the sled. The weight of their bodies set the sled in motion and it slid down the little slope. Shannon fell to her own sled and careened behind them so she could jump off when she reached the ledge and watch them as they whipped down the bigger hill.

Finley's squeals of pleasure echoed through the forest. Shannon's chest puffed out with pride. She'd thought of the idea that had turned a potentially dismal afternoon into an afternoon of joy.

She watched Finley and Rory plod back up the hill. When they reached the ledge, she stooped down and hugged Finley. "That was fun, wasn't it?"

Her eyes rounded with joy. "It was great!" She turned to her dad. "Let's go again."

"Hey, I just slogged up that hill three times. I need a break." He headed up the slope again. "But you can ride your saucer down the little hill as much as you want."

Surprisingly, Finley said, "Okay," and followed him up the slope. At the top, she set her butt on the saucer and sent herself lobbing down the hill.

Rory dropped to the snow. "I am seriously tired."

Shannon plopped beside him. "After three little rides?"

He tweaked a curl that had escaped from her knit cap. "Three *little* rides? You try walking up that hill three times in a row with no break."

Finley's final whoop of laughter as she slid to a stop on the ledge reached them. Shannon's heart swelled again, filled with warmth and joy. This was what it would feel like to have a real family. A loving husband. An adorable child.

Watching Finley trudge up the slope with her saucer, Rory said, "This is why I love having a kid. The fun. When Finley's not in a mood, she can be incredibly fun." He peeked at Shannon. "And spontaneous. The things she says sometimes crack me up."

She glanced down the hill at Finley, saw the

joy on her face, the snow on her tummy, and she laughed. "Yeah. She's cute."

Shannon's laughter filled Rory with peace. The whole afternoon had been fun, even though he'd told her about his ex-wife. Or maybe because he'd told her about his ex-wife. She seemed to feel enough sympathy for Finley that she'd gone out of her way to make his little girl happy.

"You really love Finley, don't you?"

Her question surprised him so much that he glanced over at her again. The sun sparkled off the snow that clung to her. Her full lips bowed up in a smile of pure pleasure as she watched his child—his pride and joy—pick herself up and head up the hill.

"I adore her. I love being a dad."

Her smile trembled a bit. "I bet you do."

He snorted a laugh. "You've seen the bad side of parenting in the past twenty-four hours. Most of the time Finley makes me laugh, fills in my world." He shrugged. "Actually, she makes my world make sense, gives all the work I do a purpose."

"You're a great dad."

"Yeah, too bad I won't have any more kids."

Her face registered such a weird expression that he felt he needed to explain. "When a spouse leaves the way mine did, no explanation, no trying to work things out, just a plain old 'I don't love you anymore and I certainly don't want to be a mom…'" He shrugged again, forced his gaze away from her, over to the blue, blue sky. "Well, you're left with a little bit more than a bad taste in your mouth for marriage."

"Marriage doesn't have anything to do with having kids."

He laughed. "You're right. Not in this day and age, with adoption and surrogate mothers." He caught her gaze again. "But it's difficult enough to handle Finley—one child—without a mom. I couldn't imagine adding another. So it's just me and Finley for the rest of our lives."

"Even though you love kids, you wouldn't try any of the other options?"

"Nope. But if I had a wife I would. Of course, if I had a wife I could have kids the old-fashioned way." He waggled his eyebrows, but the truth of that settled over him and he stopped being silly. "If I could commit again, I'd love to have more kids. *My* kids. A little boy who'd look like me. Another little girl who might look like her mom."

When he caught her gaze again, her eyes were soft and sad. He could have been confused by her reaction, except he knew his voice had gotten every bit as soft and sad. He'd revealed some personal tidbits that she probably wasn't expecting. Hell, even he hadn't realized he felt all those things about kids until the conversation had turned that way.

Of course, she'd sort of turned it that way.

Now that he thought about it, she owed him some equally personal tidbits. "So what about you? No husband? No kids? Married to your store?"

She brushed her hand along the top of the snow. "This time last year I was married."

"Oh?" Something oddly territorial rattled through him, surprising him. Sure, he was attracted to her…but jealous? Of a guy from her past? That was just stupid.

She batted a hand. "I got dumped pretty much the same way you did." Avoiding his gaze, she ran her mittened hand along the surface of the snow again. "One day he loved me. The next day he didn't."

"I'm sorry."

"It's certainly not your fault." She caught his gaze, laughed lightly. "And I'm over him."

"Oh, yeah?"

She shrugged. "Only a fool pines for someone who doesn't want her."

"I'll drink to that."

She craned her neck so she could see Finley again, then she faced him. “She’s going to sleep like a rock tonight.”

Rory said, “Yeah,” but his mind was a million miles away. The easy way she’d dismissed her marriage had caused his jealousy to morph into relief that she wasn’t just free, she was happy to be free. That somehow mixed and mingled with his suddenly active hormones and he wanted to kiss her so badly he could taste it.

But that was wrong. Not only had he been hurt enough to never want to risk a relationship again, but she’d also been hurt. After less than twenty-four hours in her company he knew she was a sweet, sincere woman, who might take any romantic gesture as much more than he would intend it.

Still, that didn’t stop him from wanting to kiss her. With the snow in her hair, on her jacket, covering her jeans. If he slid his hands under her knit hat, to the thicket of springy black curls, and pulled her face to his, he could kiss her softly, easily just because they were having fun.

But would she realize it was a kiss of pure happiness over the fun afternoon? Or would she make more of it?

He pulled back. They were having too much fun—Finley was having too much fun—for him to spoil it over a craving for something he shouldn't take.

He rose, put his hand down to help Shannon stand. "She'll be back any second."

"Do you think she'll want to go down again?"

"Undoubtedly."

"Hope you're rested."

He grinned. "Hope *you're* rested because I'm taking the saucer and you get the runner sled."

With that he grabbed the saucer and joined Finley at the top of the slope. Shannon pretended great interest in the sled he'd left for her, but she didn't even really see it. Her heart pounded in her chest and her insides had all but turned to mush. For a few seconds there, when their conversation had paused, she could have sworn he was going to slide his hand behind her neck and pull her forward so he could kiss her.

Kiss her!

What a crazy thing to think! Ridiculous wishful thinking on her part, that's what it was. They might be having fun with his daughter, but that was no reason for a man to kiss a woman. She was simply too much of a romantic.

But figuring all this out now was actually a good thing. Rory had come right out and said that if he married again, he would want kids.

His own kids. A son of his own. Another adorable daughter.

And didn't that sound painfully familiar? The last man she would have expected to leave her over not being able to have kids was her seemingly wonderful ex-husband. He'd loved her. She'd never had any doubt. Yet, once she couldn't give him a son—a real son, his flesh-and-blood son—he'd bolted. She wasn't sure she could handle that kind of rejection again. So she was glad they'd had this little talk early on. There'd be no more wishful thinking. No more hoping he'd kiss her.

But right here and right now, she was a lonely woman, and she had both Rory and his daughter in her yard, enjoying her company. She'd be crazy to be upset. Crazier still to withdraw just because there couldn't be anything romantic between her and Rory. The smart thing to do would be to simply relax and enjoy their company.

She picked up the sled. Studied it. Could she ride this down the slope and get it stopped on the ledge? Or would she go racing down the hill?

She smiled. Either way she'd probably make Finley laugh. So why not?

* * *

When they returned to the house, Shannon realized she hadn't taken anything out of the freezer for dinner. Her only choice was to thaw some hamburgers in the microwave and make use of the frozen French fries her mom always bought in bulk then had to give away because she and her dad couldn't eat them all.

As soon as they stepped into the kitchen, she walked to the refrigerator, removed the meat from the freezer section and tossed it on the counter. Unzipping her dad's big parka, she said, "That was fun."

Rory helped Finley out of sweater number one. "Really fun."

Finley grinned. "Lots of fun." She sat on the floor as her father tugged off her little pink boots, then helped her slide out of the first of her two pair of jeans. "But I'm hungry."

"Me, too! I thought I'd make burgers and fries."

Finley bounced up. "All right."

Rory ruffled her hair. "Go wash your hands while Shannon and I get started on the food."

She nodded and all but skipped out of the room.

Shannon unwrapped the hamburger, set it in a bowl and put it in the microwave on low.

As it hummed behind her, Rory said, "What can I do?"

"I guess we could plug in the fryer to heat the oil for the fries."

She rummaged through a cupboard beside the sink and found the fryer. After pouring in fresh oil, she plugged it in.

Rory laughed. "That still leaves me with nothing to do."

"You could go check on Finley."

"I probably should. She had such a busy afternoon that I may find her asleep on the bed."

While he was gone, Shannon hung her parka in the hall closet and took the breakfast dishes out of the dishwasher.

When he and Finley returned to the kitchen a few minutes later, Finley was carrying a little laptop. Rory joined Shannon at the counter where she was forming the hamburgers. "She can play a game or two while we cook." He pointed at the hamburgers. "How many of these should we make?"

"How many do you want?"

"I'll eat two. Finley will eat one."

"And I'll eat one." She glanced down at the plate. "We already have four. So it looks like we're done."

He nudged her aside. "I'll take it from here.

Usually I grill hamburgers, but I can use a frying pan, too."

Shannon retrieved plates and utensils and stacked them on the table. She grabbed a handful of paper napkins and set them beside the plates.

Finley glanced up. "Can I help?"

Surprised, but not about to turn down help, Shannon said, "You can arrange the plates and silver while I start the French fries."

Finley nodded. Shannon walked back to the refrigerator, removed the frozen fries and put them into the fryer.

Dinner conversation was very different from the quiet lunch. Finley chattered about how much fun she'd had sledding and how silly her dad looked on a sled. Rory reminded her that she didn't think him silly the times he rode down the big hill with her and she giggled.

Shannon basked in the ordinariness of it. A happy little girl and her father who clearly adored her. They bantered back and forth as Rory cut her burger in half and poured ketchup for her fries.

Shannon took a bite of her own hamburger. Rory was a nice guy, with a big heart, trying to raise a daughter abandoned by her mother. She supposed that was why he'd pulled away rather than kiss her that afternoon. He was too busy to be looking for a romance. But as quickly as she thought that she reminded herself of her decision not to even ponder a romance with him anyway. She'd seen the expression on his face when he talked about having more kids. A son. No matter what he said or how busy he was, someday he'd want to remarry. He'd want that family. Those kids.

And she couldn't have any.

The aching pain filled her as it always did when confronted by her barrenness. The loss. The unfairness.

For the first time in months she wanted to flirt. Wanted to be pretty to somebody—and she had to pull back.

For both of their sakes.

CHAPTER FOUR

"WELL, SHE'S ASLEEP." Rory plopped down on the sofa beside Shannon, who was pulling strands of tinsel through her fingers to untangle them. Supper had gone well. But after the dishes had been cleared, Finley had begun to nod off, so Rory had taken her for a bath. "She went out like a light the second her head hit the pillow." Rolling his head across the sofa back, he smiled at her. "You're great with her."

Shannon laughed. "Not really. In case you didn't notice my strategy, I simply kept her busy until she dropped from exhaustion."

He laughed.

"I'm serious. She's obviously a smart little girl. She bores easily. The trick to preventing tantrums might be simply keeping her busy."

"I can't always do that. I have a company to run. So it's her nanny, Mrs. Perkins, who gets the brunt of her moods. Though she spends a lot of time entertaining Finley, there are days when Finley only wants me. If she breaks down and calls me and I come home, we feel like we're rewarding Finley for bad behavior."

"You are." She turned her attention to her tangled tinsel again. She didn't like to pry, but he needed help and now that she'd spent a little time with Finley, she realized she'd learned a great deal watching her friends and their children in South Carolina. "There are lots of things you can do to discipline her. The first is to get her accustomed to hearing the word *no*. But you have to be smart about it. If she's tired or hungry, she won't take well to it. If you don't watch her mood, and discipline her when she's not open, it'll make things worse."

He tweaked her hair. "How'd you get so smart?"

She shrugged. "I pay attention?"

He laughed. "Right." He paused, obviously waiting for her to say more, and when she didn't he said, "I'm serious. I've asked you this before, but you always blew me off. And I'm curious. Did you read a book or something? Because if you did, I'd like to get that book."

"No book." She ran some more tinsel through her fingers, once again debating how much to tell him. After a few seconds, she said, "When

I lived in South Carolina with my ex, all of our friends had children. We'd be invited to picnics and outings and I'd see how they handled their kids. My husband really wanted children and I wanted to be a good mom. So I'd watch." She laughed slightly at how stupid she probably sounded. "Technically, I spent my entire marriage watching other people raise kids."

The room grew silent. Every pop and snap of the logs in the fireplace echoed in the quiet room.

Rory finally broke the silence. "So what happened?"

She peeked at him. "Happened?"

"To your marriage."

Once again, she thought before answering. There was no way she'd tell him the truth. It was humiliating to be deserted by the man you loved on the day you needed him the most. Humiliating that a man who'd truly loved her couldn't stay. Humiliating that she'd been abandoned for a physical defect.

Plus, Rory was in Green Hill to buy her store. They might be spending some personal time together because of the storm, but at the end of the weekend they would be business associates.

Still, they were stranded together and he'd

told her some personal things. So she couldn't totally ignore the question.

She ran the last of the first strand of tinsel through her fingers and began spooling it around her hand so it would be ready to hang the next day when Rory and Finley left.

"I suspect my ex was a little like your ex."

He laughed. "Really?"

"He had very definite ideas of how he wanted his life." She continued spooling so she didn't have to look at him. "He wanted things to be a certain way. When we hit a point where I couldn't make those things happen, he dumped me."

He sat forward, dropped his clasped hands between his knees, then straightened again and caught her gaze. "I'm sorry your ex was a jerk."

"I'm sorry your marriage didn't work out."

Once again silence reigned and unspoken thoughts rippled through her brain. He was a nice guy and, at her core, Finley was a sweet little girl. She'd give anything to have had a good husband and a beautiful child. Anything.

Rory leaned toward her and her heart expanded in her chest. They were only a foot apart. A shift forward by him, a shift forward by her and their lips could touch.

But uncertainty leaped in the dark depths of

his deep brown eyes. Though he didn't say a word, she knew the litany undoubtedly rattling through his head right now. They were both wounded. He had a child. And as soon as they got out of his storm, they'd be doing business. They shouldn't get involved.

He pulled back, away from her, confirming her suspicions, and disappointment shuddered through her.

He rose. "I guess I'd better head off to bed myself. I'll see you in the morning."

She smiled. "Sure. See you in the morning."

But something splintered inside her heart. Since Bryce, she'd lived with a feeling of inadequacy. Not being good enough. Never feeling womanly enough. Though Rory had good reasons not to kiss her, those feelings of inadequacy reverberated through her. Whispering like demons, reminding her that for lots of men she wasn't whole, wasn't good enough… couldn't ever be good enough.

The next morning the world was still a winter wonderland. Rory ambled into the kitchen to find Shannon sitting at the table, drinking a cup of coffee.

She smiled at him over the rim. "No Finley?"

"She's still sleeping."

"Good, then I can tell you I watched the local news this morning."

He winced. "Bad?"

She laughed. "Depends on your point of view. Raleigh's employees get another unexpected vacation day. We got another six inches of snow last night and the roads haven't been cleared from the first storm."

Rory didn't care. Finley was well-behaved, happy, for the first time in the two years they'd struggled without her mom. Another day of not looking at the store didn't bother him. Unfortunately, he wasn't the only person in this equation.

"I'm sorry that you're losing revenue."

"Funny thing about running the only department store in a twenty-mile radius. You might think we'd lose a lot of business by being closed for the entire weekend before Christmas, but the truth is we'll just be busier Monday through Friday." She smiled. "We'll be fine."

Rory got a cup of coffee and headed to the table. Sitting across from her, he noticed she wasn't wearing a lick of makeup. Her hair had been combed but not styled and the riot of curls made her look young, carefree. Kissable.

His heart cartwheeled in his chest as longing sprinted through him. But he'd already been through this in his head the night before, so he ignored the yearning in favor of the more important issue. In spite of the fact that he'd almost kissed her the night before, she wasn't upset, angry or even standoffish. She still liked having him and Finley at her home.

He picked up his coffee, drank a long swallow, then said, "How about if I make omelets this morning?"

"Oh, I love omelets!" Her face brightened in a way that shot an arrow of arousal through him. He didn't know what it was about this woman that attracted him so, but he did know that these feelings were inappropriate. She'd done so much for them in the past two days that he owed her. He shouldn't be ogling her or fantasizing about kissing her.

"I have some ham, some cheese. I'll bet there's even a green pepper or two in the refrigerator."

"Western omelets it is, then."

Yawning, Finley pushed open the swinging door. "Morning."

Rory scooped her off the floor. "Morning to you, too." He kissed her cheek. "I'm making omelets."

Her eyes widened with delight. "Good!" She scooted down. "I'll set the table."

Shannon caught his gaze, her eyebrows rising in question. He shrugged. But he knew why Finley was so helpful, so accommodating. He'd like to take credit, but he couldn't. Shannon was the one who'd so easily guided her into helping with meals and setting the table, keeping her busy so she wouldn't get bored and misbehave.

And the way he thanked her was with inappropriate thoughts of kissing her?

Not good, Rory. Seriously, not good.

Shannon chopped the green peppers and ham, while he gathered eggs, beat them in a bowl. They worked together companionably, happily, as Finley set out plates and silver. But when breakfast was over, Finley slid off her seat. "Are we going now?"

Rory looked at Shannon. Then realized what he'd done. He hadn't just turned to her for help with Finley. He trusted her. He wanted her advice.

That was not good. Not because she couldn't help, but because his reaction had been automatic. Instinctive.

"Are we ever going to get out of here?"

Shannon rose from the table, taking Finley's plate with her. "Aren't you having fun?"

Her lip thrust out. "Yeah. Sort of."

"The roads are still pretty bad," Rory said. He

walked over to her and lifted her into his arms. "Unless the snowplow comes through sometime today, we're still stuck here."

Her lower lip jutted out even farther. "Okay."

Shannon understood her cabin fever, but multiplied by about fifty. Not only was she stuck in her house, but she was also stuck with a man she was really coming to like who wouldn't want her if he knew the truth about her. Even if he was interested and asked her out, she'd never accept a date. Lying awake the night before, she'd realized that if they dated, at some point she'd have to tell him she couldn't have kids. The last man she'd told hadn't taken it so well. Just like Bryce, Rory wanted kids. Was it worth a few weeks or months of *her* happiness to put *him* in a position of having to dump her when she told him?

It wasn't. Which was why the subject of a date or romance or even liking each other would never come up, if she could help it. And why needing to keep Finley busy was such a lucky, lucky thing.

She walked over to the six-year-old. "I have an idea. I have a neighbor who lives over there." She pointed over Finley's shoulder, out the window. "She's a little bit older and her husband died last year. So when we get stranded like this, she's all by herself. Imagine being all by yourself for three days, no company, nobody to talk to."

Finley gasped and pressed her hands over her mouth. "I'll bet she's scared."

"Maybe not scared. But lonely. So, since the weather's not so bad that we can't go out, I was thinking we could bake a cake and take it to her." She glanced at Rory, silently asking for his approval as she detailed her plan. "We'd have to walk, but we could think of it as fun, like we did yesterday when we were sledding."

Rory frowned. "How far away does she live?"

"Not far," she assured him. "Just far enough that we'd get a good walk in the fresh air." She faced Finley. "So, do you want to try to bake a cake?"

"What kind?"

"I have a box mix for a chocolate cake and one for a yellow. We could make peanut-butter icing for the chocolate. Or chocolate icing for the yellow."

Finley slid out of her father's arms and to the floor. "I like peanut butter."

"So do I." She nudged Finley to the door. "Go back to the bedroom and change out of your pj's and we'll get to work."

Finley nodded and raced out of the room. Rory followed her. "I'll help her."

By the time they returned, Shannon had the box cake mix on the center island, along with a mixing bowl, mixer, eggs, butter and water.

"Give me two minutes to put on jeans and a sweatshirt and we'll get this into the oven."

She scooted out of the kitchen and into her bedroom. The bed was neatly made. The bathroom was also neat as a pin. But the Wallace family scent lingered around her. Finley's little-girl smells mixed with Rory's aftershave and created a scent that smelled like home. Family. She didn't even try to resist inhaling deeply. She might not ever become a permanent part of their lives, but she liked these two. This weekend was her chance to be with them. She might not kiss him, but she wouldn't deprive herself of the chance to enjoy them.

Once in jeans and a University of Pittsburgh sweatshirt, she ambled out to the kitchen. Finley climbed onto a stool beside the center island. "What can I do?"

"I don't know? What can you do?" She laughed.

But not getting the joke, Finley frowned.

Rather than explain, Shannon said, "Can you break eggs into a bowl?"

She glanced back at Rory. He shrugged. "There's a first time for everything."

Shannon set the bowl in front of Finley. Pulling an egg from the carton, she said, "You take an egg, like this—" Demonstrating by putting the egg against the bowl's edge, she continued, "And crack it against the edge of the bowl like this." The egg broke in half, its contents spilling into the bowl.

"My turn." Finley grabbed an egg and hit it on the rim. Miraculously, the white and yoke tumbled into the bowl. She tossed the shell beside Shannon's and clapped her hands together with glee. "I did it!"

"Yes, you did." Shannon handed her the open box of cake mix. "Take out the plastic container. We'll open it and dump that into the bowl, too."

With Shannon giving Finley the opportunity to be involved in every step of the process of cake baking, it took a long time to get the cake into the oven. They played two games of Go Fish while it baked. After lunch, they made simple peanut-butter icing, spread it across the two layers and slid the cake into a carrier.

Once again, they dressed Finley in two pair of jeans and two sweaters. When they stepped outside, the snow glowed like a million tiny diamonds. Rory carried Finley across the field that separated the two houses. They stomped the snow off their boots as they walked across Mary O'Grady's back porch to the kitchen door.

Mary answered on the first knock. Short and round, with shaped gray hair, Mary wore a festive Christmas sweater and jeans. "Shannon!" She glanced at Finley and Rory. "And who is this?"

"Mary O'Grady, this is Rory Wallace and his daughter, Finley."

As Shannon made the introduction, Rory hoped Finley wouldn't say something awful about the sweet-looking woman's sweater.

"Rory was on his way to Green Hill to take a look at the store when they were stranded on the highway and had the state police bring them to my house." She offered the cake. "Since we're all getting a little bored, we brought a cake to share."

"Well, aren't you sweet," Mary said, opening her door to invite them in. She pinched Finley's cheek. "And aren't you adorable!" She smiled at Rory. "It's nice to meet you."

"It's nice to meet you, too," he said, sliding Finley through the door. The kitchen hadn't been remodeled the way Shannon's had. Old-fashioned oak cupboards dominated the room.

A rectangular table, with four ladder-back chairs, sat in the center.

Mary fussed over Finley. "Let me help you with your jacket."

Finley glanced at her dad. Rory nodded his head slightly, indicating she should just go with it.

Unzipping Finley's coat, Mary faced Shannon. "Sweetie, why don't you put on a pot of coffee so we can enjoy that cake properly?"

Shannon laughed. "You're a woman after my own heart, Mary."

After removing her coat, she walked to the counter with the ease of someone who'd been there before. Rory watched her root through the cupboards to find the filters and coffee. She got water and measured grounds.

Mary helped Finley onto a chair. "And what can I get you to drink, sweetie?"

Rory held his breath. She hadn't mentioned the sweater, but she'd gotten a little nervous over having a stranger help her with her jacket. They weren't out of the woods yet.

Finley smiled. "Milk."

Rory breathed again, as Shannon retrieved some plates and coffee mugs from the cupboard and joined them at the table. "That'll only take a minute."

Rory faced Mary. "You have a lovely home."

She batted a hand in dismissal. "I had such plans for this, then my Joe died. And I just sort of lost interest."

"But we're hoping to have a contractor out here next summer, aren't we, Mary?"

Mary's face saddened a little more. "I thought you were leaving if you sold the store."

"Probably." She glanced at Rory, then back at Mary. "But we already looked at the books with the cupboard samples. All you need to do is finalize your choices and you can easily have the entire kitchen remodeled before fall. If you want, you can call me every night with an update or tell me your problems and I'll help you figure out how to solve them."

Mary sat beside Shannon and patted her hand. "You're very good to me."

Rory suppressed a smile. It seemed he and Finley weren't the only strays that Shannon cared for. A few times it had popped into his head that her kindness to him and Finley might be an act of sorts to keep herself in his good graces when he looked at her store on Monday. He'd dismissed that thought, but now he could totally put it out of his mind. Shannon Raleigh was a genuinely nice woman.

His heart twisted a bit. She *was* a nice woman.

And Finley liked her. If he were in the market for a romance, she'd be at the top of the candidates list.

But he wasn't looking for a romance.

The coffeemaker groaned its final release and Mary jumped from the table. "Cut the cake, sweetie, and I'll get the coffee."

In a few minutes, everyone had a slice of cake and a cup of coffee or glass of milk. They talked some more about Mary's plans to remodel her house, then Mary asked Finley about school and Finley launched into an unusually happy, unusually lengthy discussion of her classes, her classmates and recess.

Mary seemed to soak it all up, but Shannon really listened, really participated in the conversation with Finley.

When the cake was gone and the conversation exhausted, Shannon rose from the table and gathered their plates, which she slid into the dishwasher. "We really have to get going. Not only do we have to make something for dinner, but it will also be dark soon."

Mary rose, too. "That's the bad thing about winter. It gets dark too early. And with all these clouds, you can't count on the light of the moon to get you home."

Finley laughed. "That's funny."

Mary tickled her tummy. "I'm a funny lady." She pulled Finley's jacket from the back of her chair and helped her slide into it. "You can come back anytime you like."

Finley nodded.

"Just always remember to bring cake."

At that, Finley giggled.

After sliding into her parka, Shannon picked up her cake carrier and headed for the door. "I'll call you tomorrow."

"Oh, you don't have to. I'm fine."

"I know, but Mom and Dad are arriving one day this week for the holiday. So you'll be invited to Christmas Eve dinner. I'll need to give you the time."

"Sounds great."

Shannon gave her a hug, opened the door and stepped out onto the cold porch.

Carrying Finley, Rory followed her. "She's great."

Leading them down the stairs, Shannon said, "She is. But she was even funnier when her husband was alive." She peeked back at Rory. "He had a heart attack two years ago. She's really only now getting back into the swing of things."

"That's hard."

"Yeah." She caught his gaze again. "But lots of life is hard."

He knew she was referring to her divorce, which she'd barely explained. Still he could tell that life—marriage—hadn't treated her any more fairly than it had treated him. It was no wonder they got along so well. Both had been burned. Both knew nothing was certain.

They finished the walk chitchatting about nothing, making conversation to alleviate the boredom. But when they got into the house and Shannon pulled off her knit cap, throwing snow around her kitchen when she freed her hair, a knot formed in Rory's stomach.

He liked her. He wanted to kiss her so much that he'd almost acted on the impulse twice.

He didn't want to get married again. He wasn't even sure he wanted to get in a serious relationship again.

But he *liked* her.

And he wanted to kiss her.

And if he didn't soon get out of this house he was going to act on that impulse.

CHAPTER FIVE

THE SNOW ITSELF might have stopped by Sunday morning, but on Monday morning the air was still cold, the wind wicked.

They set out to get Rory's car from the interstate at seven o'clock, but discovered it had been towed—with all the other stranded cars—to a used car dealership in the next town over, so the roads could be plowed.

By the time they returned to Green Hill, the store was already open for business. When they entered the crowded first-floor sales department, color, scent and sound bombarded them. Throngs of noisy people crowded the sales tables. Red, green and blue Christmas ornaments hung from the ceiling, along with strings of multicolored lights and tinsel. The scent of chocolate from the candy department wafted through the air. "Jingle Bells" spilled from the overhead speakers.

Shannon cast a quick glance at Finley, who was being carried by her dad. Her eyes had grown huge. Her mouth was a little *O*, as if she were totally surprised or totally horrified. When she threw arms around Rory and buried her face against his neck, Shannon guessed she was horrified.

Rory held her tightly. “Finley, honey, we’ve been over this already. I told you the store would be decorated for the holiday. I told you there would be Christmas songs.”

Finley only snuggled in closer.

After the lovely weekend that had caused her to begin to bond with a man and child she couldn’t have, Shannon had promised herself she would keep her distance. No more private conversations with Rory. No more helping to discipline Finley.

But a frightened child had to be an exception to her rule. She grabbed Rory’s hand and led him in the direction of the elevators.

“Come on,” she said, ignoring the *thump, thump, thump* of her heart from the feeling of Rory’s hand tucked inside of hers. “Before you know it we’ll be in my office where, I swear, there isn’t as much as a poinsettia.”

Pushing through the crowd, Shannon got them to the elevator and immediately dropped

Rory's hand. She pressed the button for the third floor. The door closed, blocking out most of the sights and scents of Christmas, but "Jingle Bells" still piped into the little box.

Finley huddled against Rory. She wasn't upset or panicky. Just huddled. Once they got into the undecorated administrative offices she would be fine.

Shannon faced Rory. "Even though we lost the weekend, we can get down to work right away. There are four administrative departments. Buyers, human resources, accounting and advertising. If you take one day with each department, that will give you a full day on Friday to walk the store and some time for questions and explanations."

"Sounds good."

The elevator reached the second floor. "Jingle Bells" became "Rudolph the Red Nosed Reindeer." Finley looked to be getting antsy, so Shannon kept talking. "I only have four departments because I combined a lot of things for efficiency."

"That makes sense—if you've combined the right departments."

"MIS with accounting. Public relations with advertising."

He shrugged. "Should work."

The elevator pinged. Shannon sucked in a breath. Though they were entering the housewares department, it was as decorated with shiny red, green and blue ornaments as every other floor in the store. And the Christmas music? Well, that was piped everywhere, except into the administrative offices. So "Rudolph" still echoed around them.

She hurriedly ushered Rory around the tables of sheets and towels, past the shelves of small appliances, past the rows of dishes, glasses and stemware.

When they finally reached the swinging door into the administrative offices, she pushed it open with a sigh of relief. The second it swung closed behind them, "Rudolph" became a soft hum. As they hurried down the hall, even the hum echoed away.

At the end of the long, thin corridor, she opened the door that led to her office suite. Wendy was already seated at her desk.

"Good morning, Ms. Raleigh."

Shannon shrugged out of her coat. "No need to be formal for Mr. Wallace's sake. We spent the weekend together."

Wendy's eyes widened. "The whole weekend?"

Rory slid Finley to the floor and helped her

out of her little pink jacket. "Couldn't get to my car until today."

"It was a mess," Wendy agreed, scrambling to take Finley's coat and Rory's topcoat and hang them on the coat tree. "So what are you planning for today?"

"Since we're late, I'm only introducing Rory to the staff this morning. Then he can pick a department to spend time with this afternoon."

Wendy said, "Sounds good to me," but her gaze fell on Finley.

Rory put his hands on his daughter's shoulders. "She'll just come with us."

Since she'd promised herself she would distance herself from Rory and Finley, Shannon didn't argue that Finley would be bored. Instead, she set her briefcase on her desk then led the Wallaces into the hall again.

"Accounting is in the suite closest to the door. Buyers are in the next suite. Advertising and PR are in the third suite and the human resources department is on the fifth floor. They need extra space for testing and continuing education so they have half the floor. The cafeteria has the other." She met Rory's gaze. "So where to first?"

With a quick glance down at Finley, he said,

"Let's just stay behind the door for as long as we can."

Understanding that he didn't want to take Finley out into the decorations and music until he had to, Shannon said, "How about buyers then?"

"Sounds great."

She led Rory and Finley to the first door and opened it onto a narrow office with a row of desks that led to an executive office in the back. Papers were everywhere. Invoices, catalogues, samples.

Shannon faced him. "I'm sure you're not surprised that we're finalizing our spring merchandise."

He laughed. "Not in the least."

She stopped at the first desk. "Lisa, Robbie, Jennifer, Bill…" All four employees glanced up at her. "This is Rory Wallace. He's our first prospective buyer."

Everyone perked up. Superenthusiastic hellos greeted Rory. He stifled a laugh. Everybody was clearly trying to give a good first impression.

He met Missy McConnell, the head buyer, then Shannon herded him and Finley out of that office and into accounting. Five desks had been crammed into the narrow space and everyone sat staring at a computer screen.

Having already established a drill, Shannon simply introduced people as she walked by their desks. Though this group looked a little more wary than the enthusiastic buyers, Rory nodded and smiled.

In department three, advertising and PR, copy layout littered a big table in the center of a much wider main room. Employees sat at drafting table desks. The department head, John Wilder, was just a tad too happy for Rory's tastes. Finley wasn't thrilled with him, either.

"So are you going to sit on Santa's lap?"

Finley's little mouth tuned down into her perfect *U* frown. "No."

"Ah. Too old for that now, huh?"

"No, I don't believe he exists."

John laughed, but Finley tugged on Rory's hand. "I don't like it here."

Rory covered for her with a little laugh. "We've been meeting people since we arrived. She's probably ready for a break."

Shannon moved them toward the door. "That's a great idea." In the hall, she stooped in front of Finley. "How about if we go up to the cafeteria and have a soda?"

Her little mouth pulled down even farther. "I want to go home."

Shannon shot a glance up at Rory, and he

crouched beside Finley. Putting his hands on her shoulders, he said, “I told you this would be boring and you said you didn’t care as long as we went to the beach afterward.”

Her bottom lip puffed out. “I know.”

“So you’ve got to keep up your end of the bargain.”

Her lip quivered. “I don’t have anything to do while you talk.”

“Things will slow down this afternoon and we’ll stay in one department. We’ll find you a chair and you can sit and play on your computer.”

“It’s noisy when you talk.”

“It is,” Shannon agreed suddenly. “And lots of those offices don’t have room for an extra chair.”

Rory glanced up at her, mortified that she was agreeing with Finley, ruining his defense.

“So why don’t we set you up in my office? Wendy will be right outside the door, if you need anything. And I have a TV in case your computer games get boring.”

“If you have Wi-Fi, I can watch TV on my computer.”

Shannon laughed. “My screen’s bigger.”

Finley laughed, too.

Rory peeked over at Shannon again. Her

abilities with Finley were amazing. She'd said she'd babysat some of her friends' kids, but she seemed so much smarter than a part-time, fill-in caregiver.

Unless he was just lacking?

Ah, hell. Who was he kidding? Ever since Finley entered this new diva phase, he'd been behind the eight ball, playing catch up rather than proactively parenting. Shannon, an objective person, knew exactly what to do because she saw things more clearly than he did.

They walked Finley back to the office at the end of the hall. Wendy looked up as they entered. "That was fast."

Shannon said, "We took a quick introduction tour and Finley got bored. So, we've decided to let her watch TV in my office while we go up to human resources."

Wendy rose. "That's a great idea. I also think we have some cola in your refrigerator…maybe even some candy."

"No candy before lunch," Rory said.

Shannon smiled. "I should think not. We've got a great cafeteria upstairs." She caught Finley's gaze. "They make the best French fries. Give us an hour to talk with the people in human resources and I'll race you upstairs. Winner gets a milk shake."

Finley gasped with excitement. Wendy laughed and took her hand. "You two go on. Finley and I will channel surf until we find some cartoons."

When they were in the hall, Rory ran his hand along the back of his neck. "Thanks."

Shannon began walking up the hall. "For what?"

He hurried to catch up with her. "For being so good with Finley."

"Finley is a very easy child to love."

That made him laugh, but Shannon didn't join him. "You're serious."

For that she stopped. "Yes. Why are you surprised?"

He pointed at his chest. "I love her because she's mine. But this diva phase has even me backing off sometimes."

"That's because you take everything too personally."

"She is my daughter."

"Right."

"You know, we've got five whole days of entertaining her."

"I know."

"And Finley's not going to settle into your office for an entire week and just play baby angel."

That time she did laugh.

"So what do you say we form an alliance?"

She peeked at him. "An alliance?"

"A partnership. My side of the bargain is that I need help. Your side is to provide that help. It's win-win."

She laughed again.

And something soft and warm floated through Rory. He hadn't exactly forgotten what it felt like to be in the company of a woman, but he had forgotten some things. Like how everything around them always smelled pretty. Or how their laughs were usually musical.

"I love it when you laugh."

Shannon took a step back, and though she'd pulled away before, avoided him before, this morning it gave him an odd feeling in the pit of his stomach. She had a real problem with him complimenting her.

After nearly three days together he should be at least allowed to compliment something neutral like her laugh.

"Why does that make you mad?"

She started walking again. "It doesn't make me mad."

"It makes you something because you stopped laughing. Pulled away." He paused, watching her race away from him. "Now you're all but running away."

"We have work to do."

"And we also spent the weekend together. We can't spend the week behaving like strangers."

"Not strangers, just people working out a business deal."

Catching up to her, he said, "Ah, so this is your business face."

She motioned a circle in front of the bright red jacket of her suit. "This is the whole business demeanor." Then she sighed. "Look, I'm seriously trying to sell you my store. It would help if you'd forget that I love to sled-ride. And that I can't cook. And I haven't even started decorating for Christmas yet."

He studied her pretty blue eyes, which were shiny with what he could only guess was fear that something personal might cause him to walk away from their negotiations. His voice was soft, careful, when he said, "Why would that help? People who like each other usually make better deals."

She looked away. "Friendships can also backfire."

Ah. "Did you have a friendship backfire?"

"No, I'm just saying—"

"And I'm just saying relax. We like each other—" For once he didn't try to deny it. All weekend long he'd been coming to know her, getting to like her. Being trapped in her little house with a strong desire to kiss her hadn't been good. But in a store filled with people and with a business deal to discuss she had nothing to fear.

Or was that he had nothing to fear?

No matter. They were both safe.

"We got to be friends over the weekend. I've even asked for help with Finley. Surely, I should be allowed to say you have a pretty laugh."

She stiffened. Then, as if realizing she was making too much out of nothing, she drew in a breath. "Yes. Of course, I'm sorry."

"No need to be sorry. Just relax."

She smiled. "Okay."

"Okay."

They spent an hour in human resources and returned to her office to pick up Finley for lunch. In the huge, bustling cafeteria they drank milk shakes and ate French fries. But Finley tossed her head back and covered her ears when "Here Comes Santa Claus" replaced the more sedate Christmas song that had been playing.

"You know what puzzles me?" Shannon said, tugging one of Finley's hands away from her ears. "How can you watch cartoons?"

Finley's eyes narrowed.

Shannon picked up a French fry. "I mean,

they're not any more real than Santa. Yet you like cartoons. Wendy told me you did."

Finley's mouth scrunched up.

Shannon dipped her fry in ketchup. "So why don't you start thinking of Santa the same way you do a cartoon character?"

Finley glanced at Rory and he laughed. "It sounds perfectly logical to me."

Finley raised her gaze to the ceiling as if she could see the music.

"Listen to the words and pretend Santa is a cartoon character."

Finley's face contorted with little-girl concentration, then she smiled. "It's funny."

"Of course, it is. That's why people like to listen. It makes them laugh."

As if to prove that, Finley giggled.

Rory laughed, too. But when he realized he was laughing and Finley was laughing because Shannon had turned Finley's hatred of Christmas songs into acceptance, his laughter stopped.

This woman was really special.

Really special.

She wasn't just pretty or sexy or even really smart. She was attuned to life. People. It was as if she saw things other people missed and knew how to use that information to make everybody feel wanted, needed…happy.

He said nothing as they returned to her office and deposited Finley with Wendy. But when they entered the office for the buyers that afternoon, he noticed something that he probably could have noticed that morning if he'd been clued in to look for it. These people loved her.

"So what are you going to do, Shannon, if the store sells?"

That question came from Julie Hughes, a woman in her twenties who gazed at Shannon with stars in her eyes, as if she were the epitome of everything Julie wanted to be when she got a little older.

"I'm not sure." Shannon smiled, casually leaned her hip on the corner of Julie's desk, clearly comfortable with her staff. "This is only Mr. Wallace's first day here. He may look around and decide he doesn't want to buy us."

"He'd be crazy," Fred Cummings said, leaning back in his chair. "We make a ton of money." He pointed at Shannon. "Due in no small part to changes this woman made after her dad let go of the reins."

Shannon laughed. "I did a few things. They've only been up and running a few months."

Fred said, "Right."

But Rory got the message. Fred wouldn't push anymore because he wouldn't insult the last company president, Shannon's dad, in front of Shannon. But it was clear things hadn't always gone so smoothly at Raleigh's Department Store.

Heading back to the administrative officer, he said, "This is some place."

Though she'd downplayed her efforts in front of her staff, in the hall, away from anyone who could see, her face blossomed with pride. "Thank you."

"But I do have one really big question."

"Fire away. There's no question too sacred."

"Why are you selling Raleigh's? It's clear you love this store. You're also very good at what you do. Why would you want to give it up?"

"My parents need the money from the sale to fund their retirement."

"Right. I get that. But you love it." He paused, then asked the question that had been bothering him for the past few hours. "Why don't you buy it?"

She stopped. Faced him. "I tried. I couldn't get financing."

"Oh. Did you try finding a partner?"

"Are you offering?"

He winced. "My family doesn't partner. We either buy outright or nothing at all."

"I didn't think so."

But Rory wasn't so easily put off. "You said I'm the first person you approached. Surely there are others, investors who might consider a partnership—"

She laughed slightly. "Rory. Are you trying to talk me out of selling to you?"

"No. It's just that it's obvious to me that you're going to miss the store." He paused. When she didn't reply, he said, "There's more to this story. I need to hear it."

For a few seconds it looked like she wouldn't reply. Finally she said, "I've actually only been working at the store a year. My husband had unceremoniously dumped me and I was devastated. So I came home. I expected to sleep away the next few months, but my dad wouldn't let me." She smiled, as if remembering. "Anyway, he got me working in the store, and when he retired a few months ago, he made me company president. Nobody expected that I'd blossom the way I did. I like the work enough that I could have stayed here the rest of my life." She shrugged. "But my parents need the money, so I have to move on. But, on the bright side, at least now I know what I want to do with my life."

"Run another store?"

"Maybe. Or maybe just head up the buyers."

She smiled. "Or the advertising department, public relations…"

He laughed. "You won't be happy unless you can have your finger in every pot."

But even as he laughed, an uncomfortable lump formed in his stomach. "I feel like I'm taking away your dream."

She shook her head. "Running my parents' store is not my dream. It's just a really great job."

"So what is your dream?"

She started walking again, but he'd seen the sadness that shadowed her face.

If he wasn't taking away her dream by buying the store, something was up with her. He considered that maybe she couldn't handle another change in her life only one year after her divorce. But she was a strong, competent woman. He believed her when she said she was over her ex and the accompanying sadness from her divorce.

So what was it?

Why did he know, deep in his gut, that something serious haunted her and somehow, some way, he contributed to it?

He caught her arm and stopped her.

When he didn't say anything, she said, "Question?"

He stared into her pretty blue eyes. All the physical reactions he'd held at bay all weekend came flooding back. Only now they were combined with emotions. He cared about her. He cared about her a lot. He didn't want to take away her dreams. He *liked* her.

The urge to kiss her itched through him again and he was growing tired of fighting it. Tired of fighting the first good thing that had happened to him in two long years.

When his head lowed toward hers, he didn't try to stop himself. For the first time since his divorce, he wasn't just physically attracted to a woman. He liked her.

Their lips met tentatively, just a quick brush. But response shivered through him. Attraction. Arousal. Wonderful forgotten sensations that he'd avoided, ignored or smothered over the past two years.

He deepened the kiss, pressing his mouth against hers and though he felt her hesitate, she pressed back.

She liked him.

Just when he would have deepen the kiss, made it a real kiss, she pulled away.

Smoothing her hand along her cascade of dark curls, she turned and started up the hall again. "We should get back to Finley."

CHAPTER SIX

AT SIX O'CLOCK that night Rory and Finley stepped into a very comfortable hotel room. A double bed sat in the middle of the room, and, as he'd requested when he made his reservation, a cot for Finley sat beside the bed. As he tossed their suitcases into the closet and slid his briefcase onto the desk, the feelings from the kiss he'd shared with Shannon that afternoon still vibrated through him. Unfortunately, all those wonderful sensations were mitigated by the awkwardness afterward. Worse, he couldn't stop thinking about Shannon herself. Her future. What would she do without the store?

He might not be taking away her "dream" but he was taking away her job. And maybe her home. With only one department store in her small city, there was no other store in town for her to manage. She'd definitely have to move away.

They'd been so busy all afternoon that she'd

easily avoided talking abut her life and that kiss. But he had to talk to her again. He couldn't sit here in a hotel all night and wonder. Plus, he'd finally figured out she probably didn't want to talk about her decisions in the hallway of an office where she could be overheard.

Finley shrugged out of her jacket, but he pushed it up her arms again.

"Hey!"

He stooped down in front of her. "I have a favor to ask."

She blinked.

"You know how Shannon took us in this weekend?"

She nodded.

"Well, she did us a favor."

She tilted her head in question. "Uh-huh."

"So now we have to return the favor."

"We do?"

"Yes." He pulled in a breath. It wasn't a fabulous plan, but it was the only plan he could come up with, so he was running with it. "Shannon was supposed to decorate her house for Christmas over the weekend."

Finley's eyes grew round and large. She wasn't a dummy. She knew what was coming.

He sucked it up and just told her straight out. "But because we were in her home, she didn't decorate. She entertained us. So since we owe her for taking us in, I was thinking we should go to her house and help her do the work she would have done had we not needed her help."

He'd couched his request in such a way Finley would see how much they were in Shannon's debt. Still, she frowned. "I don't want to."

"I don't doubt that. But didn't she give you a way to think about Christmas today that made it seem easy for you?"

"Yeah."

"So, she's done us more than one favor and now we're going to repay her. That's the way life works."

Her lower lip jutted out.

He rose anyway. "Suck it up, kid. We owe her. We're doing this. And no hissy fits or diva behavior. You might not like Christmas but Shannon does and I won't spoil this for her. So we're going."

She sighed heavily but didn't argue.

He found a phone book and ordered Chinese food before shepherding Finley back to the car. They stopped for the takeout food, and were on Shannon's front porch within the hour.

She answered their knock quickly, as if she'd been standing right by the door. When she saw them, a smile of pleasure blossomed on her pretty face, making Rory realize he'd made the right choice. "Hey."

He held up the Chinese food. "I brought a peace offering."

She motioned for them to step inside. "Peace offering?"

He handed her the bags of food, and wrestled out of his topcoat. "We wasted your entire weekend. So we decided to help you decorate."

Her gaze flew to Finley. "Really?"

"Yes." He glanced down at his daughter. "Right?"

Finley sighed. "Right."

Shannon led them into the kitchen. "Well, thank you very much. I can use the help." Depositing the food on the center island, she added, "Would you rather eat first and decorate second, or eat as we decorate?"

"How about eat as we decorate?" He slid his gaze to Finley, hoping Shannon would get the message that if Finley was busy eating then she wouldn't actually have to decorate. An easy way to avoid trouble.

She nodded slightly, indicating she'd caught his drift. "I have some paper plates we can use." She walked to the cupboard to get them. "We'll make it like a picnic."

They set everything up on the coffee table between the floral sofa and twin sage-green club chairs. When it came to dealing with Finley, Shannon was fine. But when the room grew quiet and Finley was busy eating rice and sweet-and-sour chicken, shivers of fear sprinkled her skin.

He'd kissed her. Spontaneously. Wonderfully. And everything inside of her had responded. It wasn't a kiss of lust or surprise, as it would have been had he kissed her over the weekend. This kiss had been…emotional.

They liked each other. Two and a half days of forced company coupled with a day of walking through her store, finding out about each other, had taken their physical attraction and turned it into an emotional attachment.

It was wonderful…and scary…and wrong.

She knew the end of this rainbow. If they got involved—dated—at some point she'd have to tell him she couldn't have kids.

And everything between them would change. Even the way he saw her—

Especially the way he saw her.

She pulled in a breath. Told herself to settle down. If he bought the store, she would leave. If he didn't, he would leave. He'd go back to his life and company in Virginia, and she would stay here. Distance alone would keep them from dating. And if they didn't date, she wouldn't have to tell him.

So why not enjoy the evening?

Or use it as a chance to bring Finley along? No child should hate a holiday filled with wonder and magic. Her mom should be ashamed for ruining one of the best times of the year for her daughter. But in the past three days, Finley gone from being horrified about anything even related to the holiday, to actually laughing at the Christmas songs piped into the cafeteria. Maybe it was time to nudge her a little more?

Catching a piece of chicken in her chopsticks, she said, "You know, I like Christmas music when I decorate. You laughed about the Christmas songs today at lunch. So I'm just going to pop in a CD right now."

Finley glanced at Rory. He shrugged. "Just think of them like cartoons. The way Shannon told you this afternoon."

Finley sighed. Shannon found the Christmas music but kept the volume low. A soft mellow song drifted into the room. Finley turned her attention to her dinner. Wanting to get as much done as she could while Finley was cooprerative, Shannon grabbed the spools of tinsel she'd created the night before.

"I'm going to hang these from the ceiling."

Rory glanced over at her. “Is that code for I need a tall person to help me?”

She laughed. “Yes.”

He took the tinsel from her hand. She pointed at a corner. “What my dad used to do at our old house was string the tinsel from one corner to the center, and from the center to the opposite corner, making two loops. Then we’d do that again from the other corners.”

He frowned. “Why don’t you just direct me?”

“Okay. Walk to the corner, attach the tinsel with a tack, then loop it to the center of the ceiling.”

He did as she said. When they met in the center, she tacked the tinsel in place. “Now walk to the opposite corner and tack the tinsel up there.”

When the line of tinsel was in place, he smiled. “Not bad. Sort of festive.”

“Glad you like it.” She handed him another strand of tinsel. “Because now we’ve got to do the other two corners.”

He happily took the strand of tinsel and repeated the looping process.

When he was done, she offered him the ball of mistletoe her dad always put in the center. “Just hang this where the strands meet.”

He looked at the mistletoe, looked at her.

Then it hit her. The mistletoe was pretty, but it

was plastic. They'd hung the silly thing in their living room for years and, basically, no one paid any attention to the fact that it was mistletoe or the traditions that surrounded it.

Obviously, Rory wasn't so casual about it.

Embarrassment should have shot through her. Instead, when their gazes met, the warmth of connection flooded her. She really liked this guy.

But she'd already figured out that they weren't right for each other. Plus, once he made a decision about her store, they'd never see each other again. They had no time to form a deep emotional attachment. There'd be no time for a real commitment. They'd spend so little time together there wouldn't even be a brush with one. Was it so wrong to want another kiss?

It might not be wrong, per se, but it did lead them down a slippery slope. A slope she might not recover from if she actually fell for him in this little span of time they had together. If they fell, and he asked her to stay or asked her to come to Virginia with him, or ask for any kind of commitment at all, she'd have to tell him.

And she couldn't do that. Not again.

She caught his gaze. "We don't have to bow to the whims of superstition or tradition."

He bounced the ball of mistletoe on his palm. "But what if we want to?"

Frissions of delight raced through her bloodstream. She couldn't stop the pleasure that blossomed in her chest. But that only made her realize how easily she could fall and how careful she'd have to be spending the next few days with him at the store.

Still, she didn't want to make a big deal out of this. She tapped his arm playfully. "Just hang the darn thing."

They hung more tinsel in her dining room and threaded it around her doorways. With the shiny silver tinsel in place, she handed Rory a box of bright blue Christmas-tree balls. "Hang these on the tinsel…about three feet apart."

"Okay." He glanced at Finley, who had finished her dinner and was sitting, watching them. He offered the box to her. "Want to hand these to me?"

She shrugged. "I suppose." She scrambled up from her seat beside the coffee table and took the box.

Shannon gathered their dishes and carried them to the kitchen. When she returned to the living room, Rory and Finley had a little assembly line going. Finley would hand him a blue ball. He'd hang it on the tinsel. By the time he turned for another ornament, Finley already had one in her hand for him.

"What do you think I should do with the drapes?"

Rory glanced over. "Do?"

"Should I loop some tinsel across the top?" She pulled some plastic fir garland from the big box on the floor. "Or maybe some of this fake fir stuff."

Finley said, "It's too green," surprising both Shannon and Rory.

"Too green?"

"Yeah. The curtains are green."

Understanding what Finley was saying, Shannon said, "Right. Maybe we should loop some tinsel around the garland so it stands out a bit."

"Or just put up lights."

"Lights!" Shannon said, liking that idea. "My parents left me all kinds of lights." She rummaged through the box of ornaments again. She presented two sets. "What do you think? Little twinkle lights or these bigger lights that don't blink?"

"I think you'll see the bigger ones better."

Rory laughed at Finley's answer. "When did you become an expert?"

Finley's nose wrinkled. "What's an expert?"

"Someone who knows what she's doing," Shannon replied. "You're a natural."

Finley shrugged. But Shannon dug out the bigger lights. With her hands full, she kicked a stepstool over to the front window.

But before she could climb up to reach the top rod, Rory was behind her. "Need help looping those?"

She turned so quickly that she nearly bumped into him. Warmth exploded through her. So did ridiculous need. She didn't remember ever being so spontaneously attracted to a man. But she was to him. And she'd already decided it was wrong. Or pointless. Or both.

She stepped back, putting some necessary space between them. "Just loop them across the top."

Finley ran to the step stool. "I'll help."

Rory laughed. "You're certainly enthusiastic suddenly."

She shrugged. "This is kinda fun."

Shannon ruffled her hair. "I told you."

As Rory and Finley strung the brightly colored lights across the top of the drapes, Shannon rummaged for more decorations from the boxes her parents had left behind when they moved to Florida. She pulled out figurines of two kids skiing and figurines of people sledding and set them out on the end tables. She found a gold table runner and set it on the coffee table with red and green candles.

Seeing Rory and Finley were still stringing the lights, she decided this would be a good time for her to make some cocoa and headed for the kitchen. But she'd barely gotten the milk in the pan before Rory walked in.

"After the way you shot me down over the mistletoe, I'm guessing I should apologize for kissing you this afternoon."

His comment surprised her so much that she turned from the stove. The repentant look on his face squeezed her heart. Because she'd been as much of a party to that kiss as he'd been, she'd be a real hypocrite if she let him take the blame. "No apology necessary."

"Really? Because you're kind of standoffish."

She drew in a breath. What could she say? *There's no chance of a relationship between us, so I'm being careful?* She'd look like an idiot. Especially since in this day and age a kiss didn't necessary equate to a relationship. Hell, for some people sex didn't necessarily equate to a relationship.

"I'm tired."

"Yeah, me, too." He took a few more steps into the room, walking to the center island, where she'd set three mugs on a tray. "What's this?"

"Mugs for cocoa."

He glanced up. Smiled. "I love cocoa. I haven't had it since I was about eight."

"Then it's time you did."

He laughed. "That's exactly why I didn't want to apologize for kissing you. I wanted to kiss you."

Pleasure exploded inside her again. Why did he have to be so sweet? "Because I make cocoa?"

"Because you make me laugh. You're a nice person. A good person. I'd be an idiot if I didn't see how you're turning Finley around. She's actually humming a Christmas song in there."

She walked over to the stove, stirred the cocoa mix into the warm milk. "I'm not really doing much of anything. I think Finley's finally ready to be turned. I just have more Christmas things at my disposal than you do."

He shook his head. "No. I think she's ready because you nudge her along."

She walked to the island, brusquely picked up the tray of mugs to take to the counter by the stove. But he caught her hand. "Why won't you let me compliment you?"

"Because I'm not doing anything. It's the season. The time she's spending at the store." She shrugged, wishing he'd let go of her hand so she could scamper away. Wishing he'd hold on to it because it felt so good to have a man touch her again. And not just any man. Someone she liked.

"Well, we're at the store because of you…so we're back to you being responsible."

Humor crinkled the corners of his eyes, pulled his full lips upward. Her heart stuttered a bit, filled with hope. How easy it would be to simply laugh and accept what was happening. Part of her longed to do just that. To relax. To enjoy. No matter what he decided about the store, they'd separate. She didn't have to fear getting involved in something so deep it would force her to tell her big secret.

But the other part knew that she couldn't spend another four days with this man without falling head-over-heels in love. She was so needy, so desperate, that every scrap of attention he threw her drew her in like a kitten to a bowl of fresh milk. She had to keep her distance.

Still, she argued with her wiser self. Couldn't she enjoy this, breathe it in, savor it…so she'd have pleasant memories for the long cold nights ahead?

She didn't know. If in her desperation she fell

in love, those wonderful memories she was creating could actually haunt her.

So she simply shrugged. "I see myself more as having fun with Finley than being responsible for her turnaround."

"And we are a team."

She smiled slightly. She'd forgotten they'd formed a team that morning. "You're right."

"Seriously, you're great with kids. You're going to make a wonderful mother."

Tears sprang to her eyes. His comment wasn't out of line. It wasn't even unusual. But she hadn't been prepared for it.

She yanked the tray of empty mugs from the center island, effectively pulling her wrist out from underneath his hand and scurried to the stove to grab a ladle to scoop hot cocoa into the mugs.

"Want to get the marshmallows?" she asked, her voice cracking just a bit.

He pulled away from the center island. "Sure. Where are they?"

She pointed. "Second shelf, second cupboard."

He opened the cabinet door and pulled out the marshmallows.

"Grab a bowl from that cupboard over there," she said, pointing at a cabinet across the room.

"And put about a cupful in the bowl. That way you and Finley can take as many marshmallows as you want."

He filled the bowl with marshmallows, set it on the tray in the center of the three cups of steaming cocoa. But he didn't move his hand so she could lift the tray.

So she stepped away again. "You know what?" She walked to the refrigerator and opened the door of the small freezer section on top. "I have some Christmas cookies from a batch I made last weekend." She retrieved a plastic bag of fruit horn cookies. "Since Finley's handling the Christmas music, maybe it's time to indoctrinate her into cookies."

He laughed. "They don't look like Christmas cookies."

But when she brought a plateful of the cookies to the microwave to thaw them, he was in her way again.

She edged past him, first to get a plate to lay them out on, then to open the microwave door. When she set the timer and turned away, once again he was right in front of her.

"My little girl had lost Christmas and you're helping her find it again."

"*We're* helping her find it again," she pointed out, reminding him of the team they'd formed.

"It's more you." As he said the words, his hands fell to her shoulders and his head descended. She realized his intention about two seconds before his lips met hers, but by then it was too late to pull away.

Sensation exploded inside her. Sweet, wonderful need. Her arms ached to wrap around his shoulders. Her body longed to step into his, feel the total length of him pressed up against her. But fear shadowed every thought, every feeling. What would he say if she told him she couldn't have kids? How would he react? Would he be so loving then? Or angry as Bryce had been?

She swallowed. She didn't want to test him.

Still, there was no need. They'd really only just met. In a few days, they'd part. Couldn't she keep the situation so light that there'd be no worry about falling in love?

Maybe.

Hope bubbled up inside her. They also had a built-in chaperone in Finley. He wouldn't go too far in front of his daughter. Since he was so persistent and she couldn't seem to evade him, maybe she should just enjoy this?

It felt incredibly wrong to be wishing a relationship wouldn't last. Even more wrong to bask in the joy of the knowledge that time and distance would ultimately part them. Right at that moment, with his lips brushing hers and sweet sensation teasing her, she didn't care. For once in her life she wanted to think of herself.

That resurrected her wiser self. Even in her head the voice she heard was hard, scolding. *Your life is not as simple, your problems not as easily solved, as other women's. You cannot be flip.*

Just when she knew he would have deepened the kiss, she pulled away. Sadness bumped into anger and created an emotion so strong, so foreign she couldn't even name it.

But she did know she was mad at her wiser self.

You are such a sap. Such a scaredy-cat sap. Surely you can kiss a man, be attracted to a man, enjoy a man without thinking forever?

The answer came back quick, sharp. *No. You can't.*

She made the mistake of catching his gaze as she stepped back. The confusion in his dark orbs made her swallow hard. But she comforted herself with the knowledge that it was better for both of them if she didn't explain.

She picked up the tray. "Let's get this cocoa to Finley before it's cold."

CHAPTER SEVEN

TUESDAY MORNING Shannon walked through the employee entrance of Raleigh's Department Store a nervous wreck. After the kiss debacle, Rory had gone quiet. He'd enjoyed his cocoa and allowed Finley to drink hers, but he hadn't stayed after. He'd just gone.

Absolutely positive she'd blown her opportunity to spend time with Finley—and that she didn't need to have any more internal debates about how to handle their attraction because she'd pretty much killed any feelings he might have been having for her—she was more than annoyed with her subconscious. Especially when she'd fallen asleep and had a wonderful dream about them. The three of them. Not just her and Rory married, but her and Rory raising Finley.

She walked through the dark, silent first floor of Raleigh's. The light coming in from the big front windows reflected off the shiny oversize Christmas ornaments hanging from the ceiling and lit her way to the elevator. Inside, she pressed the button for the third floor and drew in a long, cleansing breath.

Watching herself interact with a child, even in a dream, had intensified her yearning for her own little boy or girl. She'd awakened with a tight chest and a longing so sweet in her tummy that she knew beyond a shadow of a doubt that she needed to adopt a child. Or maybe two children. Or maybe a whole gaggle of kids. In her gut, she knew she was made to be a mom. Since Mother Nature had stolen her normal child-getting avenue away from her, she would simply go an alternative route.

That solid, irrevocable decision was the good effect of the dream. If she wanted to be a mom, she could be.

But…

Now that she was so sure she would become a mom, shouldn't she want to spend as much time as she could with children? Especially one-on-one time like the kind she got with Finley? And shouldn't she also want to spend time with parents, the way she had in South Carolina? Learning the ins and outs of the things they did automatically. Rory might have stumbled a bit dealing with Finley the Diva, but he did so many things automatically, instinctively. Like get her coat. Slide her little arms into sweaters. Make sure she had ketchup.

She'd been watching other people with kids her entire adult life, preparing to become a mom. Now that she had up-close-and-personal time with a daddy and daughter, wasn't she stupid to throw it away?

She licked her lower lip and remembered every second of both kisses Rory had given her. She remembered the flash of heat that accompanied the sweet, romantic caresses. She remembered the yearning to step into his embrace, the longing to wrap her arms around him, and knew it would be risky to her heart to spend any more time with him.

But just as quickly, she reminded herself that she wasn't weak. In the past year, she'd lost a part of herself, then lost her husband because she wasn't whole anymore. She'd come home. Taken over her family's store. Gotten over her pain.

Surely, she could direct a relationship between herself and Rory away from romantic to a place where they could be friends.

Of course she could. She was strong. Her problems had made her strong. Now that she had sorted all this out in her head and had a solid course of action, she was even stronger. More determined. With her mind set, she could spend a lifetime in his company and not waver.

She walked into her dark, quiet office. Turned on the light. She could do this. She *would* do this.

Twenty minutes later, Rory and Finley strolled in. Finley raced over to her desk and gave her a hug. "I had fun last night."

Closing her eyes, she squeezed the little girl affectionately. Without Finley she might have taken years to make her decision to adopt. For as much as Rory thought he owed her with Finley, she knew she owed Finley more.

"I had fun last night, too."

Shannon rose and helped Finley out of her jacket. "Did you bring your laptop?"

Finley nodded.

"I have a surprise." She lifted a new video game off her desk. "I bought you a game."

Finley's face lit up. "What is it?"

She glanced at the CD. "I'm not sure. Something with frogs and dragons. Wendy said her grandkids love it."

Finley eagerly took the game Shannon handed her.

Shannon laughed and faced Rory. "So what do you want to do today?"

Obviously avoiding her gaze, he shrugged out of his topcoat. "Chat with the people in advertising and public relations."

She pressed her intercom button. "Wendy, we're ready for you to help Finley install her new game. Mr. Wallace and I will be with advertising."

Wendy said, "Great," and within seconds was in the doorway to Shannon's office.

Shannon walked around the desk and headed for the door. "She's all yours." She pointed at Rory. "You come with me."

Rory swung Finley up and gave her a smacking kiss goodbye. "We'll be back in time for lunch."

Finley said, "Okay," then slithered down.

As Rory and Shannon walked out, Finley eagerly raced to Shannon's chair, where Wendy sat booting up her laptop.

In the hall, Rory glanced over at Shannon. The night before, she'd acted very oddly with him, refusing to let him compliment her, getting nervously quiet after he'd kissed her. He didn't need to be hit on the head with a rock. She didn't want him kissing her.

So that morning in the shower, he'd given himself a stern lecture. Kissing her had been wrong. Her reaction to the mistletoe should have clued him in, but he was so damned sure his charm and good looks would smooth things over that he'd made a mistake. A big blunder. But this morning he would fix that by apologizing.

Except, she didn't seem to need an apology. She seemed strong and in control. No moodiness. No nerves.

He could have been insulted by the second, annoyed that she was denying the attraction he knew hummed between them, but he wasn't that much of an idiot. He might be feeling the stirrings of being interested in a relationship, but it was clear she wasn't. His divorce was two years in the past. Hers was one. He was incredibly physically attracted to her. She might not be incredibly attracted to him. He liked her. She… Well, he might not be as charming as he'd always thought.

Plus, they were together because of a business deal. Once the deal was done, she might feel differently. She could be standoffish right now because she wanted to get a fair price for her store. And if she did like him, if she was only pulling back because of their business deal, wouldn't he be an idiot to push her?

Of course, he would.

When she reached the door marked Advertising, he hustled in front of her and grabbed the knob. It certainly wouldn't hurt to start being a gentleman, and show her his charming, likable side, while they were doing business so that once their business was concluded he might be able to ask her out.

Even the thought sent a ripple of excitement through him. He couldn't believe he'd spent two long years on his own. But he had. And that was probably for the best. But now, he was ready.

She smiled at him as he walked through the door and his heart swelled with ridiculous hope. She obviously wasn't holding a grudge against him for kissing her. He had three or four days left for him to mend his reputation, show her he was a nice guy, and then, when the deal was done, he could pounce.

Good God, he liked having a plan!

John Wilder, obviously having been alerted by Wendy, stood in the center of the big room. "What would you like to see first?"

"Actually, I'd like to talk first." He glanced around the room. "With everyone."

John's brows rose. "Individually?"

He laughed. "We have all day. And I'd like to get a good feel for what this division does to justify its existence."

John straightened with affront. “You can’t have a department store without ads in the local paper.”

Rory laughed. “Relax.” He glanced at a red-haired woman who was the only one in the department still working. “I’d like to start with her.”

She glanced up, pointed at her chest. “Me?”

“Yes. You are…”

“I’m Rose.”

“And you do what?”

“Layout mostly.”

“Great. Where can we talk?”

John gestured toward a small conference room and Rory motioned for Rose to join him there.

Unusually comfortable with Shannon, Rory didn’t think twice about the fact that she was always with him when he made his visits, until she stepped into the conference room with him and Rose. It was only day two of his tour, but he suddenly realized that he’d never once been alone with anyone from her staff. Worse, he hadn’t once questioned the fact that Shannon stuck to him like glue. Normally, he’d ask for time on his own. Time to see the store. Time to get the real scoop from employees. Yet, with Shannon, he’d never even thought of it.

By eleven o'clock they'd interviewed everyone and were back in John's office. At the end of that time he'd also concluded that he'd never questioned Shannon's continuing presence because he liked her and he liked spending time with her. But even friends checked up on each other's facts and figures in a business deal. He'd been so preoccupied with the personal side of their relationship that he'd fallen down on the job. He might not insist she back off from his department visits just yet, but before this week was out, he'd get some private time with everyone. He'd also spend the evening on the internet, checking things out even more. Then, in the morning, before he came to the store, he'd talk with some of her vendors.

"So are you ready to break for lunch?"

Jarred out of his reverie, Rory said, "Yeah. Sure."

John rose from his seat. Papers of various and sundry kinds and sizes littered his desk. "Why don't I come with you? We can continue our discussions over a hot roast beef sandwich?"

Rory was about to decline with an apology, but Shannon beat him to it. "That would be great, but Rory has his daughter with him. She's been stuck in my office all morning. I don't think we should bore her with business."

John easily backed off. "I'll see you after lunch then."

Shannon said, "Great."

But Rory kept himself a step or two behind her as they walked out of the advertising offices, concerned that she'd answered for him. Normally, he wouldn't care, except the night before she'd been so quiet. And today she was all but bursting with confidence.

Of course, she was trying to sell him her company. And from what he'd seen of her dealings with staff, she was a take-charge person.

His libido instantly wondered how that would play out in bed and in his head he cursed himself. It was that kind of thinking that had gotten them to this place. He'd already promised himself that he wouldn't make another move, wouldn't say another inappropriate word until they had this deal done. And he wouldn't.

When they entered Shannon's office, Finley was deep in play. Striding over to the desk, he said, "Hey, aren't you ready for French fries?"

She didn't take her eyes off her computer screen. "Just one more minute."

He glanced over at Shannon and the look of love on her face for his little girl nearly did him in. How could he not fall for the woman who loved his daughter? Especially when her own mom hadn't?

He sucked in a breath, told himself to think about this later and said, "Come on, Finley. I have lots of work to do this afternoon. We need to go now."

She sighed heavily, but got off the chair and scampered over to Shannon, who took her hand and led her out of the office.

A strange sensation invaded his chest. Four days ago, he thought he'd never see his normal daughter again. But a little bit of time with Shannon had changed everything.

And he wondered if that wasn't a big part of why he liked her so much, why he was so ready suddenly to jump into another relationship.

Was he really seeing Shannon romantically or was he only falling for her because he wanted help with his daughter?

They walked through the cafeteria line, choosing their lunches, and when Finley picked whipped-cream-covered cherry gelatin and pie as her main course, Rory simply took those dishes off her plate and told her to choose again.

But Shannon smiled and said, "I'll bet your dad would let you keep the gelatin as your dessert if you picked a better main course."

Frowning, Finley studied the available food.

Finally, she took a salad and an order of fries. But Rory stared at Shannon. He remembered that they'd formed an alliance. He'd been the one to suggest it. But his question about his motives in wanting a relationship with Shannon came back full force. He suddenly felt as if he were using her. And, even worse, that he might be thinking of Shannon romantically just because he wanted a mother for his child.

Nerves skittered down his spine. What if he was? Oh, lord. What if he was?

Then he was scum.

They found a table in the back and once Rory opened Finley's little packet of ranch dressing and poured it on her salad, she started to eat. Her mouth full of lettuce, she said, "I really like the game, Shannon."

Shannon and Rory both said, "Don't talk with your mouth full."

Shannon quickly looked down at her own salad, but those odd feelings floated through Rory again. It was wonderful to have a partner. Wonderful to have backup. With Shannon around, it wasn't just him against Finley. He had an ally.

Finley chewed and swallowed then said, "I also forgot to say thanks."

The guilty sensations bombarding him intensified. That morning he should have prompted Finley to thank Shannon and he'd forgotten. He was proud as hell that Finley had remembered, but it served as yet another reminder that he wasn't as good with Finley as he needed to be. And he was getting comfortable with Shannon picking up the slack.

Shannon said, "You're welcome. It was my pleasure. I appreciate you being so patient while I show your dad my store."

Kicking her feet under the table, Finley grinned.

Rory's heart about burst in his chest. Not from love or even pride. From some hideous emotion he couldn't name. He didn't have to ponder or think this through. Finley liked Shannon. She liked having a woman around. Having a woman around settled her. Was it any wonder he was interested in Shannon? Any wonder he wasn't demanding to see her store on his own? He wanted to stay in her company and in her good graces. He didn't want any friction between them so she'd continue to help him with Finley.

He was double scum.

Once they returned Finley to Shannon's office and Wendy's care, they started up the hall to the advertising department again, but Rory stopped her by placing his hand on her forearm.

"Wait."

She turned, smiled. "What?"

"I want some time alone with the people in advertising."

She didn't hesitate, her smile didn't slip. "Sure. No problem. I understand that you'd want to see what they'd say when the boss isn't around."

"And I think I'd like to be by myself tomorrow when I spend the day with accounting."

Again, her smile didn't slip. No hesitation when she said, "Sure." Her smile actually grew. "I'll be happy to spend this afternoon and tomorrow with Finley."

His heart lurched. She really did love Finley.

"And I also thought it would be a good idea for the two of you to come to my house for a little more decorating tonight."

She might not have hesitated, but he did. He wasn't at all sure that was a good idea. Except, he was confused about his feelings for Shannon and maybe a little private time would clear everything up for him?

"Are you sure we're not an imposition?"

She laughed her wonderful musical laugh and his heart about kicked its way out of his chest.

How could he ever worry that he only wanted to spend time with Shannon because she was a good mom to Finley? He *liked* her. God, if he liked her any more he wouldn't be able to hold off telling her until after he made a decision about the store.

"I love having you around."

He caught her gaze and found himself trapped in her pretty blue eyes. "Thanks."

"You're welcome. And don't bring food. I'll cook."

He chuckled, glad she'd said something that could bring him back to reality. "Thought you couldn't cook?"

"I wasn't thinking anything fancy. Just macaroni and cheese and hot dogs. Things Finley might be missing since you're on the road."

His heart expanded again. She was so good to Finley that it was easy for him to see how he could be confused. But he wasn't confused anymore. She was beautiful. Smart. Fun. He liked her.

Ha! Take that, Fate. He *liked* her.

He frowned. Great. He liked her. But he couldn't tell her or make a move until after their deal was done. And he was about to spend private time in her company. This night might not be the piece of cake that he thought.

* * *

That night when they arrived at Shannon's house, she opened the door and welcomed them inside, proud of the scent of macaroni and cheese and hot dogs that greeted them.

Impatient while her dad helped her out of her jacket, Finley cried, "Hot dogs!"

"Yep. And macaroni."

"All right!"

She turned to take Finley's jacket and saw Rory shrugging out of his coat and she did a double take. He wasn't wearing his usual dress shirt and dress pants. Instead, he wore jeans and a T-shirt. She'd seen him in jeans, of course, but that was over the weekend when everything was awkward. Tonight he looked so relaxed, so casual in her home, that her pulse fluttered.

She sucked in a breath. Reminded herself she could do this. For the opportunity to spend time with Finley, she could be with Rory without giving in to her attraction.

"Right this way."

She led them into the kitchen and walked directly to the stove. Pulling a tray of hot dogs from the broiler, she said, "Everything's ready. Take a seat."

At the table, Rory put a hot dog on a bun for Finley, who eagerly bit into it. "This is good!"

Shannon took a quick swipe over her mouth

with her napkin to keep from scolding Finley for talking with her mouth full. Rory had been giving her odd looks all day. It had taken a while but she'd finally figured out that she might be overstepping her boundaries by constantly mothering Finley. Whether he'd asked for help or not, she was just a bit too helpful. So it was best to back off a bit.

She served yellow cake for dessert then accepted Rory and Finley's help clearing the table. When the kitchen was cleaned, she turned from the sink and said, "Okay, everybody, let's get our coats on."

Rory's eyebrows rose. "Coats?"

"We're going to put up the outside lights."

Finley clapped. Rory frowned. "It's dark."

"I know. But my dad has a big spotlight that we can use." She laughed. "It'll light up the whole yard."

"Setting up seems like it will take more time than the actual decorating."

"I know. But my parents will be home soon. And I was going to do this last Saturday—" She paused. She didn't want them to help because of a guilt trip. "Never mind. I didn't mean that like it sounded. I only meant that I was running out of time."

But it was too late. Rory said, "Of course, you're right. We'll set up the big light and decorate."

After shrugging into his coat and assisting Finley with hers, Rory followed Shannon out to the shed behind her house. Though they'd been there on Saturday to get the sleds, he took a closer look this time around, as Shannon dug through a mountain of junk stored in her shed.

"What is all this?"

She peeked up. "My parents had no use for a lot of their things when they moved to Florida." She pointed at a snowblower. "Especially winter things." She went back to working her way through boxes and containers. "So they left it all with me."

He looked around in awe. "I'm not sure if I envy you or feel sorry."

"Feel sorry. Because if I have to move to a warmer climate when I sell Raleigh's, I'm going to have to have a huge yard sale. If I stay in snow country, I've gotta move all this stuff to whatever city I end up in."

He laughed.

"Ah-ha! Here it is." She struggled to get the big light out of a box and he raced over to help her. Their gloved hands brushed and though

Rory felt an instant connection, Shannon didn't even react.

Which was fine. They were wearing gloves. Besides, did he really expect her to have heart-racing, pulse-pounding reactions every time they touched?

Hoisting the light out of the box, he frowned. *He* was having heart-racing, pulse-pounding reactions around her. It only seemed fair that she would have them, too.

After they set the light on the floor, she scrambled away. "I have an extension cord."

He glanced over his shoulder and saw that she held a huge, orange heavy-duty extension cord.

She grabbed the neatly bound electrical cord of the spotlight and connected it to the extension cord. "I'll unwind as you walk out to the yard. When the cord stops, that's where the light sits. Anything that isn't lit by the light doesn't get decorated."

He chuckled. "Sounds like a plan."

He walked out into the snowy front yard. When he ran out of extension cord, he unwound the light's cord and went another ten feet.

"That's it!" he called and Shannon and Finley came out of the shed. Shannon held a huge roll of multicolored lights. Finley skipped behind her.

"I'd like to put these around the porch roof."

He glanced over at it. "We'll need a ladder."

She motioned with her head to the shed behind her. "It's on the wall. I'll turn on the spotlight."

He easily found the ladder and when he carried it out of the shed, he quickly noticed two things. First, the spotlight could illuminate a small village. Second, she and Finley sat on the porch steps, laughing, waiting for him.

He stopped walking. He loved that she was so affectionate with Finley, but right now, dressed in simple jeans and her dad's big parka, with the flood light making her hair a shiny sable and her big blue eyes sparkling, he liked *her.* He liked everything about her. He even liked that she'd sort of conned him into helping her with the big job of outdoor decorating.

And he was getting a little tired of pretending. A little tired of holding back. He'd waited two long years to find somebody else. He didn't want to wait another ten minutes to enjoy her. He wanted her now.

He headed to the porch again. Since they'd already proven that they could be professional at work even though they had a totally different connection outside the office, he was going for it. He might not seduce her or even kiss her, but tonight by his behavior he would show her that he liked her. And if he was lucky he might even force her to admit she saw him as more than a potential purchaser for her store.

And after that, let the chips fall where they may.

He thumped the ladder against the porch roof. "Okay," he said, huffing just a bit because the ladder was heavy. "I think we need an assembly line. Put the lights on the porch."

Shannon turned and set the big roll of lights on the floor behind her.

"Finley, you stand by the roll and carefully unwind them as Shannon feeds them to me."

He grabbed the ladder, jostled it to be sure it was steady, and said, "I'll be up here."

He paused, faced Shannon. "Once I get up there, is there something to hang the lights on?"

"The previous owner left her hooks. They're about six feet apart."

He started up the ladder. "Perfect."

He looped the string of lights on the first hook on the right side of the porch and strung them on hooks until he couldn't reach the next one. Then he climbed down to reposition the ladder.

At the bottom of the ladder, he smiled at Shannon. She quickly looked away.

Deciding he'd simply caught her off guard, he moved the ladder over to the center of the porch, climbed up and hung the rest of the lights. When he came down, Shannon skittered away from the ladder.

Okay. He hadn't imagined that, but she could be eager to get done, not in the mood for tomfoolery.

He brushed his gloved hands together, knocking the roof dust and snow from them. "What now?"

"Now, I have a Santa's sleigh to set up in the front yard."

He peered at her. "Really?"

"Hey, my dad loves Christmas. It would be a disappointment for him if we didn't set up the sleigh."

"Okay."

They walked into the shed and Shannon went directly to a lump covered by a tarp. Flinging it off, she revealed a life-size Santa's sleigh, complete with a plastic life-size Santa.

Finley crept over. "Wow."

Rory laughed, amazed that things Finley used to hate now amused her simply because Shannon got her to relate to Santa the same way she did cartoon characters.

She turned to him with wide eyes. "It's so big."

"Yeah, it is," Shannon agreed. "But my dad loves it."

Rory walked over. He knocked on the sleigh and confirmed his suspicions. "It's plastic."

"Yeah. That's how I know we can lift it." Shannon faced him, so he smiled at her.

She quickly turned away. "Anyway, it's light. Won't be hard to carry out. We just have to anchor it."

Disappointment rose, but he smashed it down. They were working. She was single-minded in her determination to get the house and yard decorated for her dad. She wasn't rebuffing him as much as she was simply focused.

Once they got into the house, he'd be better able to gauge her mood.

They worked like a well-oiled machine. Rory took one side of the sleigh. Shannon took the other. Because Rory was walking backward, Finley directed their steps. When they had the sleigh set up, they brought the reindeer out and lined them up them in front of the sleigh. Shannon arranged small red and green floodlights around the big plastic sleigh and turned off the huge spotlight.

Multicolored lights twinkled around the porch. Santa's sleigh sat in a flood of red and green light. Finley jumped up and down, clapping her hands. Shannon looked extremely pleased that the decorating was done. And he was feeling downright jolly himself. Now that the work was done, they could play. So he reached down, grabbed two handfuls of snow, patted them into a ball and threw it at her.

She turned just in time to see it and ducked. "Hey!"

"Hey, yourself." He reached down again, grabbed more snow and tossed it before she could react. This snowball thumped into her thigh.

Finley screeched with joy and bolted behind Santa's sled for cover.

Shannon brushed idly at the snow on her jeans, glanced over at him and casually said, "You want a war?"

He motioned with his hands for her to bring it. "You think you can beat me?"

Rather than answer, Shannon bent, scooped snow and hurled a snowball at him. He dived behind an available bush. But that only gave

Shannon time to scoop up two more handfuls of snow and heave them at him.

She was good. Fast. Having been raised in snow country, she seemed to have a system down pat. And Virginia boy that he was, he didn't quite have the technique she did.

The battle lasted no more than five minutes and ended when he saw Finley shiver.

Walking out from behind the bush, he raised his hands in surrender. "Finley's cold."

Shannon thwacked one final snowball into his chest. "You lose."

"Hey, I'm from the south. Considering that we get about two snows a year, I think I held my own."

She laughed.

And his heart did a small dance. He'd been correct. She'd missed all his smiles and cues because she was focused on decorating. But things would be different now that they were done.

When he reached the porch steps, he caught Finley's hand and slid his other arm across Shannon's shoulders. She immediately slid out from underneath it.

Running up the steps, she said, "I'll make cocoa!"

Finley scrambled after her.

But Rory stayed at the bottom of the steps.

What the heck was going on here? He wasn't so bad at reading signals that he was misinterpreting Shannon's. She felt something for him. He knew she had.

He frowned. *Had.* Maybe *had* was the operative word? Maybe they'd *had* fun over the weekend, but she didn't feel anything more, anything deeper?

CHAPTER EIGHT

WALKING INTO Raleigh's Department Store the next morning, Rory had the unshakable feeling that whatever he and Shannon had been feeling for each other over the weekend, it had slipped away.

Disappointment lived in his gut. But with his gloved hand wrapped around Finley's much smaller hand as they walked through the brightly decorated store, he reminded himself that he had a child who was his first priority and a potential store purchase that was his second. Sure, Shannon was the first woman in two years to catch his eye, but she clearly wasn't interested.

He had to be a man and accept that.

He walked into Shannon's office with Finley in tow and she jumped off her seat. "Finley! I've got a great day planned for us."

He should have been happy that she was so

eager to amuse his daughter while he worked, except he had the weird feeling that their roles had flipped. She now liked Finley more than she liked him.

Which was cute and nice, but he felt like last year's handbag. A must-have when it was in style, totally forgotten now that it was old news.

Finley skipped over. "What are we going to do?"

"Well, first I have to get some work done. But that should only take me a couple of hours. After that I thought we'd go outside and stroll through the park. So you can see a bit of the city." She glanced at Rory. "If that's okay."

If her eyes shone a bit, it was over the prospect of having fun with Finley. Not because she was happy to see him, or tremblingly aware of their chemistry.

"Sure. It's fine." His heart beat hollowly in his chest. There was no more doubt in his mind. If she'd ever felt anything for him, she'd rejected it. He took off his topcoat, hung it on her coat tree, walked over to Finley and stooped down in front of her. "You be good for Shannon."

She nodded. "I will."

Shannon rounded her desk. "I'm sure she will, too."

Rory peeked up at her. Her pretty black hair

spilled around her, a tumble of springy curls. Her blue eyes sparkled with happiness. She was, without a doubt, one of the most beautiful women he'd ever seen. And she was sweet. Nice. Smart. Fun.

An ache squeezed his heart. He'd lost her even before he'd had a chance to fully decide if he wanted her.

Realizing that was probably for the best, he gave Finley another reminder to behave then headed for the accounting department. An examination of the books confirmed what he'd suspected from looking at the annual statements she'd sent him. Raleigh's Department Store made a lot of money even when her dad ran it. But profits had leaped when she'd taken the reins.

At noon, he ambled back to Shannon's office suite. Wendy wasn't at her desk, so he walked back to Shannon's office, only to discover Shannon wasn't there, either. With a sigh, he strolled to the window and gazed out. The city below bustled with activity. Silver bells and tinsel on the streetlamps blew in the breeze. The gazebo in the center of the little park looked like it was wearing a white snow hat. The city was small, comfortable. It would be a good place to raise a child. And, if he bought this store, he'd need to spend so much time here for the first three or four years of ownership that it might be a good idea to move here.

"She's happier than I've ever seen her, you know?"

Wendy's unexpected comment caused his heart to jump. He spun from the window. "Excuse me?"

"Shannon. The past few days she's been happier than I've ever seen her. She came back from South Carolina broken. Genuinely broken." Wendy paused for a second, then shook her head. "Whatever her husband did to her, it was devastating. She doesn't talk about it, but she didn't have to. It was easy to see he broke her."

Indignation roared through him. He'd like to find the bastard and give him a good shaking.

"Then you came along. Spent that snowy weekend with her and she came in that Monday different." She smiled. "Happy. Whatever you're doing, keep doing it."

He snorted. "She might have started off enjoying my company, but she's been a bit standoffish lately."

Leaning against the doorjamb, Wendy shrugged. "I told you. Her ex really hurt her. I don't blame her for being cautious." She glanced at the floor then caught his gaze. "I just… Well, she'd be crazy not to like you and I can see from the way you look at her that you're interested and…" She sucked in a breath. "Just don't give up, all right?"

Giving up was the last thing he wanted to do. Especially since he now knew she was cautious. Not standoffish. Not disinterested. But cautious. For heaven's sake. All this time that he'd been jumping to conclusions, he'd missed the obvious one. A bad divorce had made her cautious. He nearly snorted with derision. He of all people should have recognized the signs.

Finley suddenly appeared in the doorway. She pushed past Wendy and ran over to him. He scooped her off the floor. "Hey."

"Hey! They have a candy store. And a toy store."

Rory met Shannon's gaze over Finley's head. "You took her to see the competition?"

She laughed. "They're fun, interesting shops."

"I'll bet."

Unbuttoning her long white coat, Shannon said, "They really are. And because they're unique and interesting they bring shoppers to town. Those same shoppers buy their one unique, interesting Christmas gift for the year at one of the specialty shops, then they come to us for the normal things like Christmas pajamas, tea sets and trucks."

He slid Finley to the floor. "Makes sense." His entire body tingled with something he couldn't define or describe.

It wasn't fear, though there was a bit of fear laced in there. He should be as cautious as Shannon. His heart had been stomped on, too.

It wasn't excitement, though he couldn't deny that every time he saw her his stomach flipped or his heart squeezed or his chest tightened.

It wasn't anticipation, though how could he not feel a bit eager at the fact that Shannon didn't dislike him? She was simply being cautious. Wendy had more or less given him a green light and now that he had it he didn't know what to do with it.

How did a man woo a woman who'd been hurt?

Finley tugged on his hand. "Shannon said that if it was okay with you we could go shopping with her tonight."

"Shopping?" He laughed lightly, so uncertain about what to do or say. He knew exactly what Shannon was feeling. The hurt of rejection. The sting of not being wanted, not being good enough anymore for the person who took a vow to love you. He knew how shaky she felt.

He'd felt it, too. But attraction to her had quickly gotten him beyond it. Unfortunately, that hadn't left him a road map for how to help her. "Why would a person who owns a department store need to go shopping?"

"For a Christmas tree," Finley answered.

The words came out through a giggle and something that felt very much like a fist punched into his heart. Finley, the child he firmly believed would never experience the joy of Christmas had her joy back. Shannon was responsible for that. Her generosity of spirit was part of the reason he'd fallen for her so hard and so fast.

So maybe he should show her he could be generous, too? "Wendy, would you mind taking Finley into your office for a minute?"

Wendy reached down and took Finley's hand. "Sure. No problem." Very astutely, Wendy closed the door as they walked out.

Cautious himself now, Rory caught Shannon's gaze. "I'd love to go tree shopping, too…if you really want us."

She caught his gaze, smiled sheepishly, hopefully. "There's a huge difference between going tree shopping as a single adult and going tree shopping with a little girl who is seeing the holiday for the first time."

Boy, didn't he know that? Technically, this

would be *his* first time of seeing the joy on Finley's face when she walked through a forest of evergreens and chose the perfect one to sit in their big front window, so the whole town could see the lights.

He felt his own Christmas spirit stir, remembered the first time he walked into the woods with his dad to get the family's tree, remembered decorating it, remembered seeing it shining with lights on Christmas morning. His heart tugged a bit.

He swallowed. She wasn't just changing Finley. She was changing him. "All right, then. We're happy to go with you."

Shannon insisted they take her big SUV to the Christmas tree farm on the top of the hill outside of town. Without streetlights, the world was incredibly dark. A new storm had moved in. Though it was nothing like the storm that had stranded Rory and Finley at her home the weekend before, it blew shiny white flakes in front of the SUV's headlights.

She pointed at the big illuminated sign that said Wendell's Christmas Trees. "Take the next right."

Rory smoothly maneuvered the SUV onto the slim country road. After a minute, the lights of the farm came into view. A minute after that she directed him to turn down the lane. Snow coated the firs that formed a tunnel to a bright red barn that was surrounded by four white plank outbuildings. Floodlights lit the area. Cars were parked wherever appeared convenient. Some in front of buildings. Some at the side of the lane. Tree shoppers walked the thin lines between the rows of tall, majestic firs.

They stopped in front of the first outbuilding. Rory helped Finley out of the car seat they'd installed in the back of Shannon's SUV for her. She glanced around in awe. "Wow."

Rory stooped down in front of her. "I'm going to let you walk until you get tired. But as soon as you get tired, you need to tell us. It's too cold to be out here too long."

Even as he said that a gust of wind blew away the tiny white flakes of snow that glittered in his hair and fell to the shoulders of his black leather jacket. Shannon watched, mesmerized. He was so gorgeous, yet so normal.

He rose and took Finley's hand. "So how do we do this?"

Shannon took Finley's other hand. "We get a tag from the cashier over there." She pointed at a young girl who stood in front of a table holding a cash register. "Then we walk down the rows until we see a tree that we like and we tag it. One of us goes out to get one of the helpers to cut down our tree while the other two stay with the tree." She looked around at the large crowd of tree shoppers. It might not have been such a wise idea to wait until this close to Christmas to choose her tree. Of course, with last weekend's storm she hadn't had much choice. "Since they're busy, this might take a while."

Finley grinned. "I don't care."

Rory laughed. "Yeah, *you* wouldn't. If you get cold or tired, somebody's going to carry you."

She giggled.

Shannon laughed, too. Not just because of Finley but because Rory was such a good dad. So easygoing with Finley and so accepting of her limitations.

After getting a tag from the cashier, they headed into the first row and Shannon drew in a deep breath of the pine-scented air.

Rory reverently said, "This is amazing."

Shannon glanced around, trying to remember what the tree farm had felt like to her the first time she'd seen it. Tall pines towered around them. Snow pirouetted in the floodlights illuminating the area. The scent of pine and snow enveloped them.

She smiled. "Yeah. It is amazing."

He glanced over. The smile he gave her was careful, tentative. A wave of guilt washed through her. She'd been so standoffish with him the past two days that he probably thought she hated him.

"Did you come here often as a child?"

"Every year with my dad." She laughed, remembering some of the more memorable years. "He always had a vision of the tree he wanted. Some holidays it was a short, fat tree. Others it was a tree so tall it barely fit into our living room."

He smiled. "Sounds fun."

"It was." She swallowed. After her behavior the past two days, he would be within his rights to be grouchy with her. Actually, he could have refused to take this trip with her. Instead, here he was, with his daughter, ready to help pick out a tree and carry it into her house for her.

With a quick breath for courage, she said, "What about you? Did you have any Christmas traditions as a kid?"

"Not really traditions as much as things we'd pull out of a hat every year to make it special or fun."

"Like what?"

He peeked over at her. "Well, for one, we'd make as big of a deal out of Christmas Eve as we did Christmas. My mom would bake a ham and make a potato salad and set out cookies, cakes, pies and then invite everyone from the neighborhood." He chuckled. "Those were some fun nights. We never knew what to expect. Sometimes the neighbors would have family visiting and they'd bring them along. Some nights, we'd end up around the piano singing carols. One night, we all put on our coats and went caroling to the people on the street who couldn't make it to our house for some reason."

"Sounds fun."

"It was fun."

He said the words as if he were resurrecting long-forgotten memories and it hit her that he'd been left that Christmas two years ago as much as Finley had been. She wondered how much of his own Christmas joy had been buried in the pain of the past two years.

"Tell me more."

"After the big shindig on Christmas Eve, you'd think Christmas day would be small potatoes, but my mom always found a way to make it special." He laughed. "I remember the year she tried to make apple-and-cinnamon pancakes."

"Sounds yummy."

"Only if you like charcoal. She got it into her

head for some reason or another that they'd taste better if she didn't use the grill but fried them in a frying pan the way her mom used to when she was little."

"Uh-oh."

"She couldn't adjust the temperature and most of them burned. At one point the pan itself started burning." He shook his head and laughed. "I've always been glad my dad was quick with a fire extinguisher."

Finley began swinging their arms back and forth. Rory took another deep breath of the pine-scented air. A small shudder worked through Shannon's heart. It was the perfect outing. Just like a mom and dad with their daughter, they walked the long thin rows, looking for the tree that would make their living room complete. And every time they'd start walking after pausing to examine a tree, Finley would swing their hands.

"What about this one?"

Rory had stopped at a towering blue spruce. Shannon studied it critically. "You don't think it's too tall?"

"Better too tall than too short. If it's too tall, we can always shave a few inches from the bottom."

She looked at it again. The needles were soft

but bushy. Healthy. The branches were thick. There were no "holes," as her father would say. No places where you could see the wall behind the tree because there was no branch filling in the space.

"I like it."

"Then let's tag it," Rory said, reaching out to grab a branch and attach the tag. His arm brushed against her and Shannon jumped back. When their gazes met, she immediately regretted it.

He was so good to her, so kind and she was nothing but jumpy.

She swallowed. "I'm sorry."

He pulled away. "You're just nervous."

That sounded like as good of an excuse as any. Especially since it was true. He did make her nervous. He made her shaky and antsy and all kinds of things because she liked him. Still, she didn't need to tell him why she was nervous.

"It's cold. It's close to Christmas. I have lots of work to do." She shrugged. "So, yes, I'm nervous."

He cast a quick glance down at Finley, who was preoccupied with fitting her little pink boot into the footprint of someone who had walked down the row before them. "You're not nervous because you like me?" He smiled endearingly. "Not even a little bit?"

His question was so unexpected that she pulled her bottom lip between her teeth, stalling, trying to figure out what to say. She didn't want to insult or encourage him.

Finally, confused and out of her element, she said, "I'm not sure."

He laughed. "You like me."

Her breath stuttered into her lungs at his confidence. She was on the verge of denying it, like a third grader confronted by the cute guy in class and too afraid to admit her crush, but he didn't give her time.

He turned and faced Finley. "Want to stay with Shannon or walk back with me so that we can get one of the tree cutters back here to help us out?"

She didn't even hesitate. "I'll stay with Shannon."

He gave Shannon a wink before he turned and headed down the row. Finley said, "I like your tree."

Shannon glanced down with a smile. "I do, too."

"My dad picked out a good one. He's smart."

"Yes, he is smart," Shannon agreed, but her throat was closing and her knees were growing weak. He hadn't confronted her about liking him to give her a chance to argue. He'd made a statement of fact, then walked away, as if giving her time to accept it.

Accept it?

She *knew* she liked him. She fought her feelings for him every day. He hadn't needed to tell her. He hadn't needed to get it out in the open for them to deal with.

She sucked in a breath. Stupid to panic. In another day or two, he'd be done looking at her store. Then he'd leave. And the rest of their dealings would be done through lawyers. Even if they had to meet to sign an agreement, it would be at a lawyer's office.

They wouldn't spend enough time together for her "liking him" to mean anything. Even if he liked her back.

Which he did—

Oh, dear God. That's why he'd said that! He was preparing her to hear him tell her that he liked her.

With a glance down the row, she saw Rory returning with the tree cutter. She moved Finley out of the way as they approached.

As if he hadn't just dropped the bombshell that threatened to destroy the entire evening,

Rory said, “You can go down and pay if you want.”

She nodded, and, holding Finley’s hand, she raced down to the cashier. She paid for the tree and directed Finley to the SUV, where Rory and the farm employee were tying her blue spruce to her vehicle’s roof.

As they got inside the vehicle and headed home, Shannon and Rory were quiet. But Finley chatted up a storm.

“So how do we get the tree in the house?”

Rory said, “We’ll park as close as we can to the porch, then I’ll hoist it on my shoulder and hope for the best.”

Finley giggled. Shannon almost laughed, too. She could picture him wobbling a bit with an entire tree on his shoulder.

“And then what do we do with it?”

He looked over at Shannon. “I’m guessing Shannon has a tree stand.”

“What’s a tree stand?”

Shannon took this one. “That’s the thing that holds up the tree. Since it doesn’t have roots anymore, it needs help standing.”

Finley nodded sagely. “Oh.” Then she grinned. “Do we get hot cocoa after that?”

“As much as you want.”

Rory peeked over at Shannon. "But not so much that she's too wired to go to sleep tonight."

An unexpected longing shot an arrow straight to her heart. She wanted them to stay the night. She wanted to put the tree up in the living room, make hot cocoa and decorate the tree with them. Not just Finley, but Rory, too. She'd liked his stories of happy Christmas Eves and Christmases. She liked that his mom couldn't cook any better than she could. She liked that he didn't mind telling stories of his past. She liked that he didn't mind leaving her with his child, doing the heavy lifting of the tree… Who was she kidding? She also liked that he was good-looking, funny, smart—and that he liked her.

She turned to look out the window. *He liked her.* Her heart swelled with happiness, even as her stomach plummeted. He could like her until the cows came home, but that didn't change the fact that they wouldn't ever be together.

Pulling into her driveway, Rory said, "I think the easiest way to get the tree off the SUV is for me to stand on one side, while you stand on the other. You untie your side of the ropes first. I'll do mine second. Then I'll ease the tree off on my side."

"Sounds like a plan."

Finley leaned forward. "Yeah. Sounds like a plant."

Rory laughed. "She said plan. It sounds like a plan."

"But a tree is a plant!"

Shannon slanted him a look. "She's got you there."

They got out of the SUV laughing. Rory stood on the driver's side, while Shannon stayed on the passenger's side.

"Okay," he called. "You untie the ropes on your end."

As quickly as she could, Shannon undid the ropes currently holding the tree to her side of the SUV.

"Okay!"

"Okay!" Rory called back. "Now, I'll untie mine."

The branches of the blue spruce shimmied a bit as he dealt with the ropes. Then suddenly it shivered a little harder, then began to downright shake. Before Shannon knew what was happening, it rolled toward her, and then tumbled off the roof.

Finley screamed and raced up the porch. Shannon squealed and jumped out of the way, but the tree brushed her as it plopped into the snow.

Rory came running over. In a move that appeared as instinctive as breathing, he grabbed her and pulled her to him. "Oh, my God! Are you all right?"

Even through his jacket she could feel his heart thundering in his chest. Feel his labored, frightened breathing.

"It just brushed me." She tried to say the words easily, but they came out slow and shaky. It had been so long since a man had cared about her so much that he hugged her without thinking, so long since she'd been pressed up against a man's chest, cocooned in a safe embrace. Loved.

She squeezed her eyes shut. There it was. The thing that scared her about him. He was tumbling head over heels in love with her, as quickly as she was falling for him. She'd spent days denying it. Then another two days avoiding it, thinking it would go away. But it wasn't going away.

They were falling in love.

CHAPTER NINE

RORY PULLED THE TREE UP and hoisted it over his shoulder the way he'd told Finley he would.

Shannon watched him. Her heart in her throat with fear that he might hurt himself, then awe at the sheer power and strength of him. He might work in an office all day, but he was still a man's man. Still strong. Masculine. Handsome.

Oh, Lord, she had it bad.

And the worst part was, he knew.

Thanking God for the built-in chaperone of Finley, she scrambled up the stairs behind him. She could hear Finley's little voice saying, "Okay, turn left, Daddy." She squealed. "Duck down! Duck down! You're going to hit the doorway!"

Shannon quickened her pace.

Rory dropped the tree to the living-room floor with a gentle thump. He grinned at her. "You women. Afraid of a little bit of dirty work."

Shannon glanced down at the pine needles around her feet. "A little bit of dirty work? I'll be vacuuming for days to get these needles up."

Rory laughed. "Where's your tree stand?"

"It's by the window."

He made short order of getting the tree in the stand. After removing her boots and coat, Finley stood on the club chair nearby giving orders. "It's leaning to the left."

He moved it.

"Now it's leaning to the right."

They were so cute, and it was so wonderful to have them in her house, that her heart filled with love. Real love. She knew beyond a shadow of a doubt that she had fallen in love with them. Especially Rory. Finley would grow up and move on. But she could see herself growing old with Rory.

And that was wrong. Really wrong. So she ducked out of the living room for a minute or two of private time in the kitchen.

Busying herself with making cocoa for Finley, she chided herself. "So you're falling in love. Big deal. He's gorgeous. He's good with his daughter. And—" She sucked in a breath. "He likes you, too. Is it any wonder you're being drawn in?"

The kitchen door swung open. Rory walked in. "Are you talking to yourself?"

Her blood froze in her veins. This was a consequence of living alone for the past few months. She did talk to herself. Out loud.

Hoping he hadn't heard what she'd said, only the mumbling of her talking, she brushed it off. "Old habit." Turning from the stove to face him, she said, "Not a big deal."

Then she looked into his eyes, saw the attraction she'd been denying and avoiding, and her pulse skittered. What she wouldn't give to be able to accept this. To run with it. Step into his arms and look into his eyes and just blatantly flirt with him.

As if reading her mind, he walked over, caught her elbows and brought her to him. "Thanks for tonight. Finley had a great time and I did, too."

His entire body brushed up against hers, touching, hinting, teasing her with thoughts of how it would feel to be held by him romantically. Her heart tumbled in her chest. Her brain said, *Say you're welcome and step away,* but her feet stood rooted to the spot. She'd longed to be wanted for an entire year, yearned for it. And here he was a whisper away.

"Do you think we should have a little conversation about what I told you at the tree farm?"

Her tongue stayed glued to the roof of her mouth. Little starbursts of possibility exploded inside her. But her brain rebuked her. *Step away. Pretend you don't understand what he's getting at.*

He nudged her a little closer. Her breasts swept against his chest. Their thighs brushed. The starbursts of possibilities became starbursts of real attraction, arousal. He was here. Hers for the taking. All she had to do was say a word. Or two. Or maybe even just smile.

"I know you're attracted to me." He laughed. "I haven't been out of the game so long that I don't recognize the signs." He nudged her closer still. "And I like you."

His head began to descend and she knew he was going to kiss her. She couldn't have told if it had taken ten seconds or ten minutes for their lips to meet. Caught in his gaze, mesmerized by his soft words, she stood frozen, yearning egging her on while fear stopped her.

But when his lips met hers, pure pleasure punched through her objections. Her brain went blank and she simply let herself enjoy the forbidden fruit he offered. His lips nibbled across the sensitive flesh of her mouth. Shivers of delight raced down her spine. He deepened the kiss, parting her lips and sliding his tongue inside her waiting mouth. Yearning ricocheted through her. Not just for physical satisfaction, but for everything connected to it. Love. Commitment. Family.

But she couldn't give him a family. And pretending she could, stringing him along, was wrong.

She reluctantly, painfully stepped away. The jackhammer beat of her pulse reduced to a low thud. The tingles of desire flooding her system mocked her.

Rory's voice softly drifted to her, breaking in on her personal agony. "Why are you fighting this?"

She leaned against the counter. Tears swam in her eyes. The arousal coursing through her blood competed with the anger and frustration battering her brain.

"If you're worried about the distance, about the fact that you may have to leave town if I buy Raleigh's, you could always continue working for me."

She squeezed her eyes shut as pain shot through her. He liked her enough that he was already making compromises.

"I'd have to stay in Virginia, but it's only

a four-hour drive. One week you could drive down to me, the next I could drive up to you." He chuckled. "I'd give you every Friday off. It's one of the advantages of dating the boss."

The tears stinging her eyes became a flood. He liked her enough that he was *planning a future.* A real future. One with kids and a dog and a white picket fence and a husband and wife who really would love each other until death parted them.

When she didn't answer, he walked up behind her. Slid his hands around her waist. "Shannon?"

The tears spilled over. Her heart splintered into a million pieces. Her lips trembled.

"Why are you upset, when I've already worked it all out for us?" He chuckled softly. "I can understand that you'd be afraid of starting something because of your ex. But I'm not like your ex. Not only would I never hurt anyone, but I like you. A lot. More than I ever thought I could like—"

She cut him off when she turned in his arms. Blinking back tears she let herself study his face, his fathomless black eyes, his wonderful, perfect mouth, the mouth that kissed so well.

She wanted to remember this. She wanted to remember what it looked like when a man really wanted her. With the pain shredding her heart, shattering her soul, at the knowledge that she was going to have to tell him she couldn't have kids, she knew beyond a shadow of doubt that she would never, ever get close to a man again. So she'd memorize Rory. Never forget him. Never forget what it felt like to be wanted. If only for a little while.

He tried to pull her close but she shrugged out of his hold. She couldn't handle it if he dropped his arms from around her when she told him the truth. Because she had to tell him the truth. Not only did he like her enough that she had to be fair, but she also liked him enough that she could accept nothing less from herself than total honestly.

She stepped away. Cleared the lump filling her throat. Quietly, with the burden of pain it always brought, she said, "I can't have kids."

His face contorted with confusion. "What?"

She drew a harsh breath, caught his gaze. When reality had to be faced, it was best to face it head-on. Bravely. Now that she had her bearings she could do just that.

"My ex left me the day I had a hysterectomy. I had the kind of endometriosis that compromises vital organs. I had no choice."

His features softened with sympathy for her. "I'm so sorry."

"And you love kids." Swallowing back a waterfall of tears that wanted to erupt, she turned away. "I see how you are with Finley, but we've also discussed this. The day we went sledding you told me how much fun it was to have Finley and that if—" Her voice faltered. "If you ever found someone to love again you would want more kids."

He stepped up behind her. "Those were words—"

"That was *truth,*" she shot back harshly. She didn't want him saying things tonight that he'd regret in the morning. She turned, faced him. She refused to let her misery compromise her pride. "You love kids. You wouldn't even have to say the words. Anybody who saw you with Finley would know. But you told me. You told me plainly that if you ever fell in love again, it would be to remarry…to have kids." She paused long enough to draw in some much needed air. "If we acknowledge that honestly, and stop what's happening between us now, there'll be no hard feelings. No one will get hurt because we barely know each other."

He brushed at the tear sitting on the rim of her eyelash. "Shannon…" Her name was a soft question that she didn't know how to answer.

So she shrugged away from him, swallowed and said, “Don’t. Really. I’m fine with this.”

He didn’t pull her to him again, but she still stood close enough that he brushed at the second tear. “Then why are you crying?”

For a million reasons. She wanted to say it. Hell, she wanted to shout it. Life had stolen her ability to have kids and with it slimmed down her pool of potential life partners. Her husband had dumped her. She hadn’t really been held by a man in an entire year. She’d gone through the worst situation life had ever handed her and she’d gone through it alone.

She was crying because she was tired. Alone. Afraid to hope. And when she looked at him, she hoped.

Rory drew a sharp breath, her pain was a living, breathing thing in the room, tormenting them both. He wanted to tell her he wasn’t going anywhere. That he didn’t care about having kids. That he liked her enough to explore what was happening between them, then Finley ran into the room.

“Where is everybody?”

Shannon spun away from the door so Finley couldn’t see her crying and Rory’s heart broke for her again. He longed to take her into his arms, to let her cry, but he respected her privacy.

If he did something like that, Finley would see and ask questions. But they could—*would*—talk about this in the morning.

He walked over and swept Finley up off the floor. "Hey, kiddo. Tree's up. It's time for us to go home."

"But I didn't get cocoa."

"We'll stop somewhere along the way."

"Okay."

But carrying his daughter to the front hall, strange feelings enveloped him. He remembered the day she was born, remembered walking the floor with her after her two-o'clock feedings. The memories tripped something in his psyche…a love so profound and so deep that it could have only come from the inner sanctum of his soul. Shannon would never know this. But, if he stayed with her, pursued what was happening between them, he would never know it again.

He'd never have a son. His flesh and blood. A little miniature of himself, but with complementing gifts from his mother's gene pool. He'd never teach *his* little boy how to play baseball. Never proudly introduce him around on the first tee of the country club golf course.

Selfish, he knew, but when he thought of life

without those things, something tore a hole in his lungs. He felt like he couldn't breathe.

It was a lot to be confronted with out of the blue. This time last week, he didn't believe he'd ever consider dating again, let alone having more kids. Now, he felt like he was in the raging pit of hell because he finally liked someone but she couldn't have kids. And he had to make a choice. A huge choice. A life-altering choice.

He found Finley's jacket on the chair in the living room where she'd tossed it while he'd settled the tree into the stand. He found her mittens on the foyer floor. By the time he had her dressed for outside and had shrugged into his leather jacket, Shannon walked out of the kitchen.

Quiet, but composed, she stooped in front of Finley. "Button up. It gets colder at night."

Finley nodded.

Shannon hugged her. And Rory's chest ached. Now he knew why she'd been so happy to spend time with Finley. Now he knew why she hadn't even hesitated when they'd needed a place to stay.

She loved kids.

And she couldn't have any.

CHAPTER TEN

THAT NIGHT RORY lay awake while Finley snored softly in the cot beside his bed. Staring at the dark ceiling, he struggled with the myriad thoughts that battled in his brain. Was she right? Would he reject her, the way her ex-husband had, because she couldn't have kids?

He didn't know. He honestly didn't know. But he did know that if he followed her lead, pulled back from a relationship, as she had, he'd never be put in the position where he'd have to make a choice. Which might be why she'd been so standoffish. She liked him enough that she didn't want to put him in the position where he had to choose. Then, as she'd pointed out, neither one of them would be hurt.

He fell asleep around four and woke at seven, tired but agreeing that the thing to do would be to follow her lead. Pull back. Hold back. Don't give her hope only to snatch it away again later if he just plain wasn't ready to handle a relationship. Or, God help him, if he couldn't come to terms with never having any more of his own children.

As he and Finley walked into Shannon's office, she rose from her desk. Wearing a red dress, with bright gold earrings shaped like Christmas ornaments, she looked festive. But her smile was cautious, wary.

"So, Miss Finley, are you staying with me this morning while your dad spends some time in human resources?"

She bounced up and down. "Yes! Are we going to do something fun?"

"Well, first I have to get my morning paperwork done." She clicked on her big-screen TV. "You can watch cartoons while I do that. Then I thought we'd just take a walk in the park, get some fresh air." She stooped down in front of Finley. "There should be carolers there this morning."

"Carolers?"

"People who sing Christmas songs."

Not enthusiastic, but at least not pouting or throwing a tantrum, Finley shrugged. "Sounds okay."

Shannon rose. "Okay? It's going to be fun."

She smiled tentatively at Rory. "So you'll be back around noon?"

He swallowed. She might be cool and collected, but he knew her heart had been broken. Irrevocably. Life couldn't do anything crueler to a woman who wanted children than to deprive her of the privilege of conceiving them.

He tried to smile, but knew the effort was lacking. "Yeah. I'll be back around noon."

When he turned to go, she caught his forearm. He faced her again.

"Don't worry about me."

"I'm not..."

"You are. But I'm fine. Really. In the past year I've adjusted, and in the past week I've made some decisions about what I want to do with the rest of my life. You just do your part. Decide if you want to buy Raleigh's. And I'll take care of everything else."

He left her office with a strange feeling of finality swamping him. *She'd* made the choice. It didn't sit right, still part of him sighed with relief. He'd just come from a bad, bad, bad marriage. Until he'd met Shannon he'd all but decided never to get close to a woman again. It scared him silly to think he even wanted to try. And the first time he tried it was with a woman who couldn't be hurt, someone who needed promises up front. Promises he was too shaky to make.

So maybe Shannon was right? Maybe it was best that there be nothing between them?

He headed for human resources, but halfway to the door to housewares, Wendy called to him. "Wait! Wait!"

He stopped. Thinking she had a message from Shannon or Finley, he said, "What's up?"

"Nothing..." She sighed heavily. "It's just that Shannon came in sad this morning and I..." She winced. "I just wanted to know if something happened last night."

His breath caught, but he refused to give in to the emotion. She'd made the choice and he respected that—if only because his own failed marriage had left him so cautious that he couldn't promise that he'd give her the love she needed. Not after only a few days together.

"Nothing happened last night." Nothing that he'd tell one of Shannon's employees. But as quickly as he thought that, it dawned on him that if Wendy, her trusted secretary, didn't know why Shannon was so heartbroken then Shannon might not have told anyone.

Except him.

He felt burdened and honored both at the same time.

"I've been divorced. I know how difficult the first Christmas alone can be. Give her some space. She'll be fine."

With that he pushed open the swinging door. He spent the morning listening to the human resources director explain Raleigh's hiring policies, its wage structure, its bonus and pension plans. Glad for the distraction, he listened intently, but the second he left the big office and headed downstairs to Shannon's office, the weight of her troubles sat on his shoulders again.

When he arrived at her office, Finley raced into his arms. "We went to the park! Saw the people sing. They were funny."

"Funny?"

Shannon laughed. "One of the singers dressed up as a reindeer when they sang 'Rudolph the Red-Nosed Reindeer.' It was hysterical."

He smiled. He couldn't help it. Finley was really coming around about Christmas. If she kept this up, in a few more days she might actually like the holiday. But, more importantly, Shannon looked better. More peaceful. He knew that was due in part to Finley's company, but he genuinely believed that since they hadn't really "fallen in love" she'd very quickly gotten beyond their near-miss romance.

"So..." He caught her gaze. "Are we ready for lunch?"

She looked away. "You go on without me."

Finley whined, "Awww!!"

Shannon peeked up, smiled at her. "Sorry, but because we played all morning I have a little work I'd like to catch up on."

A combination of fear and guilt clenched in his stomach. She didn't want to be around him anymore. Or maybe she wasn't having as much fun around Finley as she seemed? Maybe having a child around was pure torture? "If Finley's a bother, I can have her sit in a room with me."

Her eyes softened. "Finley's never a bother."

And he nearly cursed. Of all the mistakes he'd made around Shannon that was probably the stupidest. It had been clear from the beginning that she loved being around Finley. He was the one with the problem. He had absolutely no clue how to relate to Shannon anymore. Probably because he knew something about her that wasn't true for most women, and he was barely accustomed to dealing with "most" women. Of course, he was clumsy and awkward around her.

But at lunch he decided that he wasn't going to abandon her. He might stop his romantic advances. He definitely wouldn't kiss her again. Those things only seemed to make her unhappy, but he wouldn't, by God, take Finley away from her in the last two days of their trip.

That evening, after they'd eaten supper in a little Italian restaurant, he loaded Finley back into the car.

"Where're we goin'?"

"Shannon's."

"All right!"

"I have no idea what she's going to be doing tonight, but whatever it is, we're going to help her."

Blissfully clueless, Finley shrugged. "Okay."

"I mean it, Finley. This might be a little hard for you to understand, but Christmas means a lot to Shannon and I don't want any tantrums if she says or does something you don't like."

"Okay."

He bit back a sigh. He couldn't be sure that Finley really got it. But he did know he couldn't let Shannon alone that night.

She answered the door wearing a bright Christmas-print apron over jeans and a red sweater. Her dark hair swirled around her sexily, but the drop of flour on the tip of her nose made her look just plain cute.

"Hey!"

She stepped away to allow them to enter.

Rory guided Finley inside. "We weren't sure

what you would be doing tonight but we suspected you might need some help." He caught her gaze, smiled tentatively. "So we're here."

She headed for the kitchen, motioning for them to follow her. "I'm baking cookies."

Finley gasped. "What kind?"

Shannon turned and caught her gaze. "Christmas cookies."

Finley frowned but Shannon laughed. "Don't you think it's about time you learned how to bake them?"

"I'm six."

Shannon headed for the kitchen again. "I know. But next year you'll be seven and the year after that eight and before you know it you'll be twelve or so and you'll want to be the one who bakes the cookies. So, just trust me."

Finley wrinkled her nose and glanced up at her father. Recognizing she might be more opposed to the work than the idea that the cookies were for a holiday she didn't really like, he said, "Well, you don't think I'm going to bake our cookies, do you?"

In the kitchen, the dough had already been prepared. Shannon had it rolled into a thin circle. Cookie cutters sat scattered along the side of the cookie dough bowl.

He ambled to the center island as Finley

hoisted herself onto one of the tall stools in front of it.

"You see these?" Shannon displayed a bunch of the cookie cutters to Finley. "We push these into the dough." She demonstrated with a Christmas-tree-shaped cutter. "Then pull it out and like magic we have a cookie that's going to look like a tree."

Finley grabbed for the tree cutter. "Let me."

Rory tugged her hand back. "What do we say?"

She huffed out a sigh. "Please, can I do one?"

Shannon laughed. "You may do as many as you like." She laughed again. "As long as there's dough."

And Rory's heart started beating again. He hadn't realized how worried he was, how guilty he felt, until Shannon laughed and some of the burden began to lift.

Finley and Shannon cut twelve shapes and Shannon removed the cookie dough from around them. They lifted the shapes from the countertop onto a baking sheet and Shannon rolled another circle of dough.

They worked like that for about twenty minutes. When Rory also joined in the fun, it took even less time to cut out all the cookies in a circle of dough. As they cut shapes and filled cookie sheets, Shannon slid the trays into the oven. Using a timer, she kept close track of their baking times and in exactly twelve minutes she removed each pan of cookies.

When they finished the last tray, Shannon walked over to the cookies cooling on the round kitchen table and said, "These are ready to be painted."

Finley frowned. "With a brush?"

"With a lot of little brushes." She brought a plate of cooled cookies over to the counter then headed for the refrigerator, where she had icing cooling. She filled four soup bowls with icing.

"Now we put some food coloring in the bowls and make different colors of icing."

Grabbing two bottles of the coloring, Rory helped her create red, blue, green, yellow and pink icing.

She carefully caught his gaze. "You're good at this."

He laughed, relieved that she finally seemed comfortable with him in the room. "It's not we're like mixing rocket fuel."

She laughed a little, too. Finley snatched a cookie and one of the thin paintbrushes lying beside the icing bowls.

Now that the cookies had baked, they'd fluffed out a bit and didn't exactly look like their intended design. So Rory said, "That's a bell."

Finley sighed as if put upon. "I know."

Hoping to cover for the insult, he said, "So what color are you going to paint it?"

"The song they sang in the park today said bells are silver. But there is no silver icing."

"Silver bells are silver," Shannon agreed. "But cookie bells can be any color you want."

"Then I'll make mine pink."

"A pink bell sounds lovely."

Though Rory had pitched in and helped cut the cookies and even create the colored icing, he had no interest in painting cookies. He glanced around. "Would you mind if I made a pot of coffee?"

Shannon peeked over at him again. This time more confidently. "Or you could make cocoa."

Rory's shoulders relaxed a bit more. If they kept this up, by the time he was ready to take Finley home, he and Shannon might actually be comfortable in each other's company again.

He found the milk and cocoa. While Shannon and Finley happily painted cookies, he made their cocoa and served it to them. They barely paused. Seeing that it would take hours if he didn't help, Rory lifted a brush and began to paint, too.

They worked until nine. When they were through, and the cookies drying on the kitchen table, Rory told Finley to get her coat while he helped Shannon clean the dishes and brushes. In spite of the goodwill that had seemed to grow between them as they made cookies, once Finley left the room Shannon again became quiet.

Rory still didn't quite know what to say. With every minute of silence that passed, a little more distance crept between them. He knew part of that was his fault. He'd only decided he was ready to date. The decisions thrown at him the night before were usually the kinds of things people discovered after months of dating. When they were comfortable and confident in their feelings.

But he understood why Shannon had told him. They were growing close and she didn't want to.

With the dishwasher humming, she dried her hands on the dishtowel and then tossed it on the counter. "I wonder if she's struggling with her boots."

He laughed. "She always struggles with those damn things. But she loves them. So we deal with it."

Heading out of the kitchen, Shannon tried to laugh, but the sound that came out of her throat was a cross between a hum and a sigh. The whole evening had been strained. Rory tried to pretend things weren't different between them, but they were. This time yesterday, he would have flirted with her. He also would have found something to do in her living room rather than watch her and Finley make cookies. He'd clearly been bored. Yet, he stayed in the room. As if he didn't trust her not to break down.

Expecting to see Finley on the foyer floor struggling with her boots, she paused when she saw the empty space. "Wonder where she is?"

Rory's steps quickened as he ran to the closet. But as he passed the living room entryway, he stopped. "Look."

She peered into the living room and there, on the sofa, sleeping like an angel was Finley. Warmth enveloped her like a soft sigh of contentment. "She's so cute."

"Yeah," Rory agreed, slowly walking toward her. Gazing down at his daughter he said, "You've done so much for her, helping her to get into the spirit of Christmas."

She swallowed. "It was my pleasure."

"I wonder what other things she might like?"

"Might like?"

"About Christmas." He glanced over. "We've decorated, made cookies. You've even gotten her to like carols. But that's just the tip of the holiday iceberg. There are lots of things she's never experienced. Now that she's open, I'd like to introduce her to everything…make her like everything so that this time next year she'll be excited for Christmas, not sad."

Shannon bit her lower lip. She knew exactly what it was like not to look forward to the holiday. She knew what it felt like to wish every day could be normal because the special days only pointed out that you had no one to share them with. "Maybe we could get her to sit on Santa's lap."

Rory laughed as if he didn't think she'd been serious. He caught her gaze again. "That's like asking a guy who's just learned to hike if he wants to try Everest."

"I suppose." But a weird, defensive feeling assaulted her. Up to this point Rory had taken every suggestion she'd given him. Now that he knew she couldn't have kids, it was as if he didn't trust her. That might have even been why he'd stayed in the kitchen with them during cookie making.

Sadness shimmied through her. She turned and headed for the closet. "I'll get her coat and boots."

"Thanks."

When she returned to the living room, Rory sat on the edge of the sofa cushion beside Finley. Shannon handed him Finley's boots. She didn't even stir as he slid them on. But he had to lift her to get her into her coat and hat. Still, though she stirred, she really didn't waken. She put her head on Rory's shoulder when he lifted her into his arms and carried her to the foyer.

Shannon raced to open the door for them. With Finley sound asleep, it was the first time they'd said a private goodbye at the door.

"Thanks for coming over tonight. Even with the extra time to teach Finley, your help cut my cookie-making time in half." She tried to give him a confident happy smile, but it wobbled. It had meant the world to her to have Finley to teach. To have people to share her cookie-making joy with. Just to have people around who cared about her. Deep down, she knew that was why he'd come, why he'd brought Finley. He now knew she was sad. So he'd tried to cheer her.

But that's all it was. The kindness of one human being to another. Not a gesture of love as it might have been the day before—when he didn't know she couldn't have kids.

The injustice of it punched through her, made her want to rail at the universe. But she didn't.

She was the one who had made the choice to tell him, and for good reason. She couldn't be angry that she had.

Rory smiled awkwardly. "We were glad to help." He cleared his throat. "You know, today, when I asked if Finley was a bother—" He cleared his throat again. "I was just worried that she kept you from getting your work done. She likes being with you. I like letting her spend time with you."

Relief rolled through her, stole her breath, thickened her throat. She whispered, "Thanks."

"So tomorrow, while I'm walking around on the sales floor, talking with staff, watching how things are done, you could keep her all day if you like."

"Yes. That would be great."

"Okay."

"Okay."

Silence ensued again. If she hadn't yet told him, she knew he'd probably try to kiss her good-night right now. Her heart stumbled in her chest. She'd hurt both of them, because she was afraid of a bigger hurt to follow.

But it had been the right thing to do.

It had to be.

Because if it wasn't, she was missing out for nothing.

She twisted the doorknob, opened the door. "I'll see you in the morning then."

"Yes."

"Drive carefully."

He nodded, gave her one last look, then walked out to the porch.

She waited until Finley was securely buckled in and Rory had jumped behind the steering wheel, before she turned off the porch light, closed the door and leaned against it. She had another entire day of Finley's company and, if she was lucky, a little time Christmas Eve morning before they returned to Virginia. She should be overjoyed.

Instead sadness softened her soul. She liked Rory. Really liked him. Probably loved him. And she'd chased him away.

CHAPTER ELEVEN

THE NEXT MORNING Rory kissed Finley goodbye before he walked out of Shannon's office to investigate the store. Dressed in jeans and a leather jacket, so the cashiers and shoppers wouldn't guess who he was, he looked so cute that Shannon felt a lightning bolt of longing. But she contented herself with the fact that she had Finley all day again.

"So any thoughts on what you'd like to do today?"

From her seat on the sofa near the big-screen TV, Finley peeked over at her. "Don't you have papers?"

She laughed. "Yes. But I came in early to review them. I'm all yours this morning. So what do you want to do? Go to the candy store again? Maybe the toy store?" she suggested, hoping Finley would say yes so she could buy her a gift. Something special. Something she knew Finley would want. And maybe keep to remember her by.

Finley sucked in a breath. “I’d sorta like to go shopping.”

“Great! Where? The toy store?”

She shook her head, sending her fine blond hair swinging. “I wanna buy a present for Daddy.”

“Oh.” Wow. She’d never thought of that. A little kid like Finley, especially a child with only one parent, probably didn’t get a lot of chances to shop for Christmas gifts. But considering Finley’s life, a more important question popped into her head. “Have you ever bought your dad a Christmas gift?”

She shook her head again. “No.”

Though her heart twisted with a combination of love and sadness for sweet little Finley, she deliberately made her voice light and teasing so Finley’s first experience of Christmas shopping would be fun. “Well, then this is your lucky day because we have an excellent men’s department here at Raleigh’s.”

Finley rewarded her with a giggle.

“Let’s go!” She caught her hand and led her to the elevator. Inside the little box with “We Wish You a Merry Christmas” spilling from the speakers, she pressed the button for the second floor. Menswear.

As they stepped out, Finley glanced around in awe at the tables of shirts, racks of ties and mannequins dressed in suits. Customers milled about everywhere, examining underwear and pajamas displayed in long tables, studying ties.

"Ohhhh."

Shannon also looked around, trying to see the store as Finley saw it. Because Finley was only a little over three feet tall, she suspected everything looked huge.

"So what do you think? Shirt? Tie? Rodeo belt buckle?"

Finley giggled.

"We also have day planners, pen-and-pencil sets for a daddy's desk and all kinds of computer gadgets in electronics, if you don't see something you like here."

"You sound funny."

"I'm being a salesman."

Finley giggled again, but out of the corner of her eye, Shannon saw Rory talking to one of the salesclerks. Grasping Finley's shoulders, she raced them behind one of the columns holding a mirror.

Finley said, "What?"

"Your dad is here."

"Oh."

"And if we want to keep your gift for him a surprise, we'll have to be careful where we walk."

Finley nodded her understanding.

They slipped to the far side of the sales floor. Customers, Christmas ornaments, racks of suit jackets, rows of jeans and walls of ties all provided good cover so that Rory wouldn't see them.

As Finley inspected a table full of dress shirts, Shannon sneaked a peek at Rory. With his hands stuffed into the front pockets of his jeans and his shoulders filling out his leather jacket, he could have been any other extremely gorgeous shopper. He chatted happily with a salesclerk, who eagerly showed him suit jackets and ties, probably expecting a nice commission.

She hated to see him disappoint the clerk, but she couldn't stop herself from watching as he took off his jacket and tried on the suit coat suggested by the clerk. His muscles bunched and flexed as he reached around and took the jacket, then shrugged into it.

"I like this one."

Shannon glanced down at Finley. "Huh?"

Finley waved a shirt at her. Folded neatly so that it fit into a rectangular plastic bag, the shirt was a shade of shocking pink so bold that Shannon had to hold back a gasp.

"That one?"

She nodded.

"Um…have you looked at any of the others?"

She nodded. "I like this one."

"It's very nice, but…um…usually men don't like to wear pink shirts."

"Why not?"

"I don't know…." And she also wasn't sure why she was arguing with a six-year-old. Rory had enough money that he didn't need a new shirt, and the pink one, the one chosen by his daughter with all the enthusiasm in her little pink-loving heart, would be a nice memento. He could keep it forever. Save it to show her when she got her first gift from her own child. Tears sprang to her eyes. It would actually be fun to see that. To remember this day. Share it with Rory. Make him laugh.

She swallowed hard. "You know what? I like that shirt, too."

She glanced up to see which cash register could take their money, and she saw Rory going to the checkout beside the row of suits. The clerk was taking information from him—probably contact information for when the trousers had been hemmed and/or alterations made—and he was pulling out a credit card.

Her heart swelled with love for him. He *wasn't* going to disappoint the clerk who'd spent so much time with him. He was actually buying something. She pressed her hand to her chest. He was such a great guy.

"You know…I don't really hate Christmas anymore."

Stunned back to the real world by Finley's remark, Shannon peeked down at her. "I was beginning to wonder about that."

Finley grinned. "I like presents."

Shannon laughed. "I do, too. I like to give them as much as get them."

Finley nodded eagerly.

"We'll sneak to that register over there—" she pointed at the register in the far corner where Rory wouldn't see them "—and pay for this, then I'm going to buy you ice cream."

"It's morning!"

"I know. But I think you've earned it."

"What's 'earned'?"

"It means that you did something nice, so I'm going to do something nice for you."

Finley grinned.

Shannon paid for the shirt and the clerk handed the bag containing the bright pink shirt to her. She nudged her head so that the clerk would give it to Finley.

With a smile, the clerk shifted the bag over to Finley. "Thank you, ma'am, for shopping at Raleigh's. Come again."

Finley giggled.

Shannon caught her hand. "Want me to carry your bag?"

Finley clutched it tightly, her little hand wrapped around the folded-down end. "I've got it."

She was quiet as they walked out of menswear and to the elevator. When they stepped inside, amazingly, it was empty.

Shannon almost hit the button for the third floor then remembered she'd promised Finley ice cream and pressed the button for the cafeteria floor.

Finley wiggled a little bit. After the doors closed, her tiny voice tiptoed into the elevator. "Some days I miss my mom."

Shannon glanced down, her heart in her throat because she didn't know what to say. It wasn't her place to talk about Finley's mom, but she certainly couldn't ignore her. "I'm sure you do."

"I don't remember her."

Stooping down in front of her, Shannon said,

"You were very small, so you probably don't remember. But you should really talk to your dad about this. I'd love to talk with you about it, but you and your dad were both part of your mom leaving." She swallowed. "And you're family. This is the kind of stuff you talk about with your family."

Her blue eyes solemn and sad, Finley nodded. "Okay."

The urge to hug Finley roared through her. Not just because she was sad, but because they were connected. They might not be family, but somewhere along the way they'd bonded. She wished with all her heart she could have talked with Finley about this. Could have eased her pain a bit. But it really was Rory's place.

Still, though she couldn't speak, she could hug, so she wrapped her arms around Finley's tiny shoulders and squeezed.

Finley snuggled against her. "I wish you were my mom."

She closed her eyes. Only with great effort did she stop herself from saying, "I do, too." Instead, she tightened her hold, pressing her lips together to stop their trembling.

The elevator bell dinged. The doors opened. Shannon rose, took Finley's hand and headed to the cafeteria. They could both use some ice cream now.

She managed to avoid having lunch with Finley and Rory. Partially because she hoped Finley would use the private time to ask her dad about her missing mom. She knew a cafeteria wasn't the best place to have the conversation, but recognized that Rory would be smart enough to stall a bit while they were in public. That would give him time to think through what he wanted to say that night when they were alone in the hotel room.

She spent the afternoon with Finley, taking her downstairs to the gift-wrap department to have Rory's new pink shirt properly wrapped in paper covered in elves and candy canes. When Rory arrived at her office around five to take Finley home, she rose from her office chair.

"So, you're ready to go?"

"Yes." He ambled into her office. "The store is fantastic, by the way. Your clerks are very cheerful."

"Hey, some of them work on commission. And the Christmas season puts a lot of money in their pockets."

He laughed. "Ready to go, Finley?"

She scooted off the sofa. "I need my coat."

Shannon walked to the coatrack. "I'll get it."

She slid Finley's arms into the jacket, her heart aching at seeing them leave. Plus, she wanted to talk to Rory about Finley asking about her mom. The need to invite them to her house that evening trembled through her. More time with Finley was a good thing. More time with Rory was tempting fate.

With Finley's coat zipped, Shannon turned her toward her dad. "See you tomorrow."

Rory scooped her up. "Yep. We'll see you tomorrow."

It was wiser to simply let them go. She could leave Finley with Wendy the following morning, track Rory down on the sales floor, and ask for a few private minutes to talk about Finley's question about her mom. That was a much better plan than asking them to her house again that night. Especially since she was decorating the tree. And that would just feel too much like a family thing.

But, oh, she wanted it.

As their feet hit the threshold of her office door, she blurted, "I'm decorating the tree tonight, if you're interested?"

Rory turned, an odd expression on his face. But Finley clapped with glee. "Yes! I want to see the tree when it's all pretty!"

He cast her a puzzled frown. "It's not decorated yet. She wants us to decorate the tree tonight."

Finley grinned. "I know."

He shrugged. "Okay." He faced Shannon. "It looks like we're happy to help. But this time it's my turn to bring food." He caught her gaze. "Anything in particular you like?"

A million sensations twinkled through her. She nearly said, *I want you to stay. I want you to love me.* But she only smiled. "I like chicken."

"You mean fried chicken?"

She nodded.

"Fried chicken it is."

She was ready for them when they arrived a little after six. Paper plates and plastic forks were already on the kitchen table, so they wouldn't have much clean up and could get right to decorating the tree.

She opened the door with a big smile, but from the shell-shocked look on Rory's face, Shannon suspected that Finley had asked him about her mom.

She hustled them inside. "I set up the kitchen table. We can eat first, decorate second."

Not thinking about her own longings, and more concerned about how Rory had handled "the" question, she shooed Finley ahead and stopped Rory short of the door.

"She asked you, didn't she?"

He rubbed his hand down his face. "About her mom?"

She nodded.

"Yeah."

"What did you say?"

"The truth. Or at least as much of it as I could say without hurting her." He sucked in a breath. "She's six. I don't want to tell her that her mom doesn't love her—doesn't even want to see her."

"Of course not."

"She was oddly accepting of the fact that Bonnie left. Almost as if she was just curious about where she was."

Shannon let out the breath she didn't even realize she was holding. "So that's good."

"Yeah. But I have a feeling bigger questions will be coming."

"Maybe."

He chuckled. "Probably."

Finley pushed open the swinging door. "I'm hungry!"

When she spun around and the door swung closed behind her, Shannon started for the kitchen, but Rory stopped her.

"Thanks."

Her eyebrows rose. "For what?"

"For being so good to her. For listening to me when I need somebody to talk about this stuff with."

"Haven't you talked about these things with your friends?"

He cast her a look. "Do you tell your friends about your divorce?"

She felt her face redden. "Not really."

"That's why it's so nice to have someone to talk to. Someone who will listen without judging."

Understanding, she inclined her head. Even though telling him about her inability to have kids had been painful, it had been nice finally to have someone to talk to.

Someone who understood.

A little bit of her burden lessened. He did understand. She might have effectively ended the romantic aspect of their relationship, but maybe she didn't need a romance as much as she needed somebody who truly understood her pain. Somebody who truly understood that sometimes life could be incredibly unfair.

She smiled at him. "I think we better get into the kitchen."

He laughed, slung his arm across her shoulder. "Yep."

The casualness of the gesture seeped into her soul. He liked her. She liked him. They were friends. Real friends, who knew the worst about each other's lives and didn't feel sorry, didn't feel put off, simply accepted and understood. She didn't have to hide things from him. He didn't have to tiptoe around her. More important, she didn't have to worry about him finding out. *He knew.* It was amazing. Suddenly freeing.

They walked into the kitchen to discover that Finley had already opened the bucket of chicken, chosen a leg and was wrestling with the container of coleslaw.

Rory said, "I'll get that."

Shannon opened the mashed potatoes and gravy. "And I'll get this." She offered the potatoes to Finley. "Would you like some of these?"

"Yes, please."

They ate dinner having a surprisingly relaxed conversation, considering that Finley had asked the big question that afternoon.

As soon as she was done eating, Finley slid off her chair and tossed her paper plate and plastic fork into the trash. She skipped to the door. "I'm going to get started."

Rory bounced off his seat. "Not without us!" He headed for the door, then doubled back and tossed his plate and plastic fork into the trash. "If you have any valuable ornaments, I'd eat quickly and get into the living room before she tries to hang them."

With that he raced away and Shannon chuckled, shaking her head. What she wouldn't give to have them as her real family.

But she couldn't. And she did have another night with them. So she rose, tossed her plate and utensils, closed the bucket, put the remaining chicken into the refrigerator and joined them in her living room.

To her relief, she found Rory stringing lights on the tree, as Finley unspooled them.

"That's going to be pretty."

Finley beamed. "Yep."

Heading to the box containing the ornaments her parents had left behind, she said, "I'll unwrap these and we can get started."

They worked in silence for the next five minutes while Rory finished the lights and Shannon carefully removed the white tissue paper from the ornaments.

When the lights had been hung on the branches and the star sat at the top of the tree, she said, "Plug them in. We'll decorate around them."

Rory plugged in the lights and the tree twinkled and sparkled, causing Finley to gasp.

Shannon said, “It’s pretty, isn’t it?”

She nodded. “Very pretty.”

Hanging the ornaments wasn’t as simple as stringing the lights. Finley wanted to know the story behind every ornament and if an ornament didn’t have a story, Shannon had to make one up.

It was ten o’clock before they got all the ornaments hung. When it was time to leave, after Finley had had sufficient time to ohhh and ahhh, Rory carried the cocoa tray to Shannon’s kitchen, leaving Finley with the instruction to put on her boots and coat.

Shannon held the kitchen door open for Rory. As they walked into the kitchen “White Christmas” was playing on the stereo.

“Oops. Forgot to turn that off.”

She reached for it as Rory set the tray on the center island, but before she could click it off, he caught her hand. “I love this song.”

“I’ll bet! With only two or three snowfalls a year, a white Christmas is probably pretty high on your wish list. But here in snow country there’s never really a happy storm.”

He laughed, then surprised her by swinging her into his arms to dance. Holding her close, he said, "It's a pretty song. A happy song. A song about someone wishing for something he might just get." He laughed again. "Don't spoil it for me."

She said, "I won't," but inside her chest her heart pounded like a jackhammer. She told herself that they were only friends. Reminded herself that having a friend, a real friend who knew her secrets and understood her, was a blessedly wonderful feeling. But the sensations rippling through her were every bit as wonderful. She wanted him to like her as more than a friend.

But she'd snuffed out that possibility, headed it off herself. Her choice.

The song ended and they pulled away. Gazing into each other's eyes, they stepped back. Their initial chemistry kicked up again, but she swung away. Carrying the tray to the sink, she laughed shakily. "Somebody who likes snow… sheesh."

"Hey. It's hard to hate something that frequently gets you a day off."

She laughed, then heard the sound of the door as he left the kitchen. Knowing he was gone, she braced herself against the countertop and squeezed her eyes shut, letting herself savor the sensation of being held by him. Danced with. Only when she had memorized every feeling swimming through her, tucked it away to pull out on snowy winter nights without him, did she turn from the sink and go out to the foyer.

Already in her little coat and pink boots, Finley snuggled into her dad's neck, preparing for sleep. Shannon stood on tiptoes and kissed her cheek. "Good night, sweetie."

"G'night."

"I'll see you in the morning?" She made the statement as a question because he'd never really told her a time or day he was leaving. Given that they were spending another night in Green Hill, she suspected he'd stop in the store in the morning.

She peeked at him expectantly.

"Yes. We'll be there in the morning. I want to see Christmas Eve sales. But we do have a four-hour drive, so we'll be leaving around noon."

"Okay."

He smiled. "Okay."

They stared at each other for a few seconds. She swore she saw longing in his eyes. The same longing that tightened her tummy and put an ache in her chest. Then he broke away and headed for the door.

When they were gone she sat in front of the tree for twenty minutes. Just looking at it. Wishing she could keep it up forever.

CHAPTER TWELVE

AFTER BUCKLING Finley into her car seat, Rory slid behind the wheel of his car, his heart thumping in his chest. Not with excitement, but with recrimination. He knew she was sad. He knew he was responsible for at least a little bit of that sadness.

But everything between them had happened so fast. Worse, he wasn't even a hundred-percent sure he was capable of trusting someone enough to love them. He wasn't steady enough on his feet to believe he should try a relationship with a normal woman. Someone as special as Shannon was too delicate to be his romantic guinea pig.

The next morning at the store, he wasn't surprised when Shannon again offered to take Finley around the store for a few hours. Needing to see to a few details, Rory shrugged. "I'll be walking around the store, too. You don't have to do this."

She smiled. "I want to."

Then she gave him some kind of head signal that he didn't quite understand. So he laughed. Which amazed him. Even as upset as he knew she was, she still had the ability to make him laugh. And to think of others.

She angled her head toward Finley and nudged twice.

He still didn't have a clue.

So he just went with the program. "Okay. You take Finley and I'll be a secret shopper again."

Finley jumped up and down. "Okay!"

They walked together to the elevator, but when he got off on the second floor, they continued to the main floor. He walked through the menswear department and poked around in the electronics and small appliances, but couldn't seem to focus. Technically, he'd seen enough the day before. He could report back to his dad that Raleigh's had a huge, faithful group of shoppers. At Christmas time, they seemed to sell goods faster than they could restock shelves.

The store had some drawbacks. It only broke even most months of the year and two months of the year it actually lost money. But Christmas made up for that. In spades.

So why did he need to walk around anymore? He didn't.

He took the stairs to the first floor and glanced around, looking for Shannon and Finley. But the store was packed with customers. He barely squeezed through the aisles on his quest to find Shannon and his daughter, but finally he saw them standing by the candy counter.

He edged his way up. "Hey."

"Hey!" Shannon turned, smiled at him. "I thought you were shopping?"

"I think I shopped enough already."

She winced. "Is that good or bad news for me?"

"I shouldn't really tell you anything because I have to report back to my dad, and he and my brothers and I have to make an official decision...but...I can't see any reason we'd shy away from a deal."

Her eyes sparkled. "Really?"

Seeing her so happy put the air back in his lungs, the life back in his heart. After everything that had happened between them, this was at least one good thing he could do for her.

"So Finley and I can go home now."

Her head snapped around. "What?"

"I'm done. We can go home."

"But I..." She paused, nudging her head toward Finley. "I didn't get to buy someone a gift."

"You did," he said. "Remember? You bought a g-a-m-e."

"I can spell, Daddy."

Rory laughed, but Shannon's face appeared to be frozen. "I just...you know...I thought we'd have the whole morning."

He glanced at his watch, then out the wall of windows fronting the store, at the heavy snowflakes falling. "I thought that, too, but look at the weather."

Shannon turned to look, then swallowed. "I thought you liked snow."

"In its proper place and time."

"Oh."

Her eyes filled with tears and Rory suddenly got it. She wanted this time with Finley. He glanced at the snow again. If anything, it seemed to be coming down harder.

He caught her gaze. "I'm sorry. Really. But if it's any consolation I can bring Finley back when my dad and I come to present our offer."

She swallowed, stepped away. "No. That's okay. I'm fine."

She wasn't fine. She was crying. *He'd made*

her cry. Guilt and sorrow rippled through him. "I'm sorry."

Finley stomped her foot. "Daddy! We were supposed to stay."

And Finley the Diva was back. As if it wasn't bad enough that he had to leave Shannon. Now he had to deal with Ms. Diva.

"Finley, it's snowing—"

"I want to see Santa!"

Shannon looked down. "What?"

"I want to see Santa. I want to sit on Santa's lap." She stomped her foot. "Right now!"

Rory had had his fill of giving in to her tantrums, but this one he understood. From the confused look on Shannon's face, he didn't think she had promised to take Finley to see Santa, but he did suspect that Finley had intended to ask her to. She'd been taking steps all along toward acclimating to Christmas and now she was finally here.

Tantrum or not, he wouldn't deny her this. "Okay."

Shannon glanced at him. "Okay?"

He shrugged. "She's been deprived too long. I think I should do this." He paused, caught her gaze again. "Want to come?"

She smiled. The sheen of tears in her eyes told the whole story even before she said, "Sure."

He directed Finley away from the candy counter. “Let’s go then.”

They headed for the elevator and the toy department in the mezzanine that overlooked the first floor like a big balcony. Santa’s throne was in an area roped off and called Santa’s Toy Shop. Shannon led the way as Finley skipped behind her.

Rory didn’t know whether to laugh or cry. In spite of the long line, Rory kept his patience as they waited. Finley was not so good. She stepped from foot to foot.

“Don’t be nervous.”

She glanced at Shannon. “I’m not nervous. I need to get there!”

Finally, their turn came. Finley raced over to Santa as if he were her long-lost best friend.

Rory snorted a laugh. “Look at her. This time last year—this time last week!—she didn’t even believe in him. Just a few days ago, she thought of him as a cartoon character. Now look at her!”

Shannon blinked back tears. “I think she’s cute.”

His heart stuttered a bit. Shannon always behaved like a mom to Finley and when he saw her tears his own perspective changed. He swallowed the basketball-size lump in his throat. “Yeah, she is cute.”

"Ho, ho, ho!" Santa said. "And what would you like for Christmas, little girl?"

"Can you really give me what I want?" she demanded.

Rory hung his head in shame. "Oh, no. This could get ugly."

Shannon put her hand on his bicep. "Just be patient. Give her a chance."

He glanced down at her, once again grateful for her support, his heart hurting in his chest. He liked her so much. But it had all happened so fast and the choices he'd have to make were too big, but the most important thing was he didn't want to risk hurting her.

Santa boomed a laugh. Glancing at Rory and Shannon he winked. "Well, I can't make promises, but I do try my best."

"Okay, then I want you to make Shannon happy again."

Santa frowned. "What?"

Finley pointed at Shannon. "That's Shannon. She's my friend. I wish she was my mother. But this morning she got sad. Really sad." Her nose wrinkled. "I even think I saw her cry." She faced Santa. "I don't want her to be sad. Make her happy again."

Santa—aka Rick Bloom, manager of the toy department—cast an awkward look in Shannon's direction. He clearly didn't know what to say.

Shannon's eyes filled with tears. Though it was strange having a child announce her sadness in front of a roomful of kids and parents waiting to see Santa, her heart looked past that and saw the small child who cared about her enough to ask Santa to make her happy again.

Rory slowly walked over to Santa. He stooped in front of Finley. "Santa actually only handles requests for gifts."

Finley's face puckered. "Why? If he can fly around the world in one night, he can do all kinds of things."

"Yeah, but—" Obviously confused, Rory glanced back at her.

Holding back her tears, Shannon went over. She also stooped in front of Finley. "Honey, all of Santa's miracles pretty much involve toys."

"Well, that's a bummer."

Shannon couldn't help it. She laughed. Rory laughed, too. Santa chuckled. The parents waiting in line with their kids laughed and shuffled their feet.

But in spite of her laughter, Shannon's heart squeezed with love. She would miss this little girl terribly. When the tears sprang to her eyes again, she rose and whispered, “Tell Santa what toys you want for Christmas. Okay?”

Finley nodded. She glanced back at Rick and rattled off a list of toys. Rory stepped over beside her. “I’ll have to remember to get all those things.”

She nodded, but turned away. Real tears burned in her throat now. He liked her. He understood her. He needed her. And his daughter liked her.

Rory’s hand fell to her shoulders. “Hey. Are you okay?”

She sniffed. “Finley’s just so sweet.”

He laughed. “Only because of you.”

Because her back was to him, she squeezed her eyes shut.

“Are you not going to look at me?”

She shook her head. If she turned around he’d see her tears and she was just plain tired of being pathetic.

A few seconds went by without him saying anything. Finally, he turned her around, saw her tears.

He looked at the ceiling then sighed. “I’m so sorry this didn’t work out.”

She swiped at her tears, aware that at least thirty parents, thirty *customers,* were watching her. Not to mention employees. People who didn't know her secrets. People she didn't *want* to know her secrets.

"It's fine. You want the store. That's why you came. To see the store." She swallowed again. "It's fine."

"Don't you think I wish it could have been different between us? I like you. But I'm more damaged than you are. I won't take the risk that I'll hurt you more."

She sniffed. Nodded. "I get it."

"I don't think you do—"

"Ho, ho, ho!"

Recognizing the voice as her father's, Shannon snapped her head up and spun around. "Daddy?"

Dressed as Santa himself, carrying a sack of gifts, Dave Raleigh strode toward Santa's throne, gesturing broadly. "I'd like to thank my helper here for taking my place for a while this morning, but I'm here now." He dropped the sack just as her mom strode over.

Dressed in a festive red pantsuit, with her hair perfectly coiffed, Stacy Raleigh said, "Silly old coot. I tried to talk him out of this but you know how he loves Christmas."

Just then Finley scampered over. Her mom smiled. "And who is this?"

"Mom—" she gestured to Rory "—this is Rory Wallace."

Her mom extended her hand to shake his. "Ah, the gentleman who came to see the store."

"Yes." She motioned to Finley. "And this is his daughter, Finley."

Stacy stooped down. "Well, aren't you adorable?"

Finley said, "Yes, ma'am."

And Shannon laughed. But she also saw her way out of this painful and embarrassing situation. She caught Rory's arm and turned him in the direction of the stairway off the Santa-throne platform. "Thank you for a wonderful visit. We'll look forward to hearing from you after the holidays."

She stooped and kissed Finley's cheek. Unable to stop herself she wrapped Finley in a big hug and whispered, "I love you," in her ear.

Finley squeezed back and whispered, "I love you, too."

Then she rose and relinquished Finley into her dad's custody. She watched them walk down the stairs, then raced to the half wall of the mezzanine and watched as they squeezed through the first-floor sales floor, watched as they walked through the door and out into the falling snow.

Her mom caught her forearm. “Shannon?”

The tears welling in her eyes spilled over. “I want to go home.”

CHAPTER THIRTEEN

SHANNON'S MOTHER deposited her in the living room, left and returned with a cup of tea. "Drink this."

Her tears now dried up, she took the tiny china cup and saucer from her mother's hands. "Did you remember sugar?"

Her mom smiled. "Yes."

She took a sip, closed her eyes and sighed.

"Are you going to tell me what's wrong?"

Her automatic response was to say, "I'm fine." But remembering the wonderful sense of release she had being around Rory after having confessed the truth, she wouldn't let herself lie, not even to protect her mom.

She cleared her throat. "I…um…told Rory that I couldn't have kids."

Her mom's eyes narrowed. "Why?"

"Because he was starting to like me and I felt he needed to know the truth."

Her mom's face fell in horror. "You scared him off?"

Oh, Lord. She's never thought of it that way. "I didn't want him to get involved in something that wouldn't work for him."

Stacy drew Shannon into her arms and hugged her. "You always were incredibly fair."

She squeezed her eyes shut, grateful that her mom understood and even more grateful that the feeling that she'd done the wrong thing had disappeared. "He's a good man who wants more kids."

"And you can always adopt—"

She pulled out of her mom's embrace, caught her gaze. "I am going to adopt."

"On your own?"

"Yes."

She hugged her again. "And you always were brave, too." She squeezed her tighter. "I'm glad."

Shannon returned her mother's hug, closed her eyes and contented herself with the fact that being around Finley had given her enough confidence that she could go on with the rest of her life. So what if it was without Rory? So what if she didn't have someone she felt connected to? Someone who made her feel special? Someone who loved her unconditionally?

Her heart broke a bit. Though Rory and Finley had helped her to make the decision to adopt, she couldn't begin looking immediately. She didn't want to associate getting a child to losing Rory and Finley. She wanted her child to come into her life when she was totally over the loss.

And she didn't think she would be for a while.

Two hours later, Rory was battling traffic on I-95, wondering why so many people needed to be out on Christmas Eve. It was two o'clock in the afternoon when people should be at home with their families.

"So, then, I kinda peeked at Santa's ear and I think I saw something holding his beard on."

Rory absently said, "You might have."

"Because it was fake?"

He glanced at her. Now that she was "into" Christmas a whole new set of problems had arisen. Her beliefs were so precarious and so fragile that he didn't want to spoil the magic. But she was a smart kid, a six-year-old, somebody who probably would have been realizing by now that Santa wasn't real.

He had no idea what to say and reached for his cell phone to call Shannon. She would know.

His hand stopped. His chest tightened. He couldn't call her. He'd hurt her. Walking out of Raleigh's he'd convinced himself that leaving was sad, but justified, because he wasn't sure he loved her and didn't want to hurt her. But that was a rationalization. He had already hurt her. In a few short days, they'd fallen into some romantic place where it didn't matter if they wanted to like each other. It didn't matter if they spent every waking minute together or thirty seconds a day—they still wanted more. They'd clicked, connected.

But he was afraid.

Who was he kidding? He was terrified.

"So was his beard fake?"

He glanced at Finley, all bright eyes and childlike smiles. "Well, you saw the real Santa come in and take over. So the guy whose lap you sat on was like his helper." A thought came to him and he ran with it. "There's a Santa in every shopping mall around the world for the six weeks before Christmas. The real one can't be in all those places. So he trains lots of helpers."

"Oh." She frowned, considering that.

A few miles went by with Rory maneuvering in and out of the traffic. He spent the time alternating between wondering if he'd told Finley the right thing and forcing his mind away from the sure knowledge that Shannon would have known exactly what to say. Then a worse thing happened. Suddenly, he began wishing he could call her tonight and tell her about this conversation.

"So if there are lots of Santas, that explains how he gets everywhere on Christmas Eve to deliver presents."

"Exactly."

"So that means not everybody gets a real Santa. Most of us get a fake!"

Panicked, Rory glanced at her. "No. No. He's a special magic guy who can go around the world all in one night. Because he's special." He floundered, grasping for words. "Magic. It all has to do with magic."

"But you told me magic is just some guy who knows how to do things really fast or by getting you to look away from what he's really doing."

Caught in the web of an explanation he'd given Finley after they'd seen a young man doing magic tricks on the beach a few months before, he wanted to bounce his head off the steering wheel. This is what he got for having a super-intelligent child. "That is true with most magic. But this is Christmas magic."

"What's the difference?"

He peered over at Finley again. Shannon would have handled this so easily. She would have told Finley the truth. And maybe that was what he needed to do. Tell her the truth. Not the big truth that Santa wasn't real. But the other truth. The truth most parents hated admitting.

"I don't know."

"Why not?"

"Because I'm a guy who buys stores and fixes them up so that they make lots of money. I'm not the guy in charge of Santa. So I'm not in on those secrets."

She nodded sagely, leaned back in her car seat. "I miss Shannon."

He struggled with the urge to close his eyes. Not in frustration this time, but because he missed Shannon, too. He swallowed. "So do I."

"She was pretty."

Gorgeous. He couldn't count the times he'd longed to run his fingers through her thick, springy black curls. He couldn't count the times he'd noticed that her eyes changed shades of blue depending upon what she wore. He couldn't count the time he'd itched to touch her, yearned to kiss her, thought about making love to her.

"She was smart, too."

He'd definitely have to agree with that. Not only was there a noticeable difference in Raleigh's income from when her dad ran the store and when she'd taken over, but she also ran that store like a tight ship. And she always knew what to say to him, how to handle Finley.

She'd thought of sled riding and baking a cake on days when he probably would have been stumped for entertainment for himself, let alone himself and a six-year-old.

A pain surrounded his heart like the glow of a firefly. He could still see her laughing as she slid down the hill on her saucer sled, hear her screams of terror that turned into squeals of delight when he forced her down the big hill on the runner sled.

His throat thickened. He could also remember the sorrow in her voice when she told him she couldn't have kids. She believed herself unlovable—

It hurt to even think that, because she was the easiest person to love he'd ever met.

He drove another mile or two before the truth of that really hit him. Not that she was easy to love, but that he knew that. How could he know she was easy to love, if he didn't love her?

Shannon's dad arrived home around five. The store stayed open until nine for late shoppers, but Santa's throne was deserted at five with a note that told children that he was on his way to the North Pole to begin delivering gifts.

In the kitchen, where Shannon and her mom were making Christmas Eve supper, he shrugged out of his coat. He'd already removed his fake beard and white wig, but his salt-and-pepper hair had been flattened against his head. He still wore the Santa suit but the top two buttons of the jacket were undone. "So what did Wallace have to say? Is he going to buy the store?"

Shannon watched her mom shoot her dad one of those warning looks only a wife can give a husband and she laughed. "It's okay, Mom. We can talk about it."

Her dad headed for the table. "Talk about what?"

"About Rory Wallace breaking our daughter's heart."

His eyes widened, his forehead creased. "What?"

Shannon batted a hand. She didn't mind talking to her mom, but her dad had a tendency to make mountains out of mole hills. "I'm fine. We just sort of began to get close while he was here and I might have taken a few things he said to heart that he didn't mean."

"Scoundrel!"

"No, Dad. It was me. We were attracted, but he sort of laid everything out on the table early on in the week. He had a wife who left him, who doesn't want anything to do with their daughter."

He fell to one of the chairs at the table. "Oh."

"Then he mentioned a time or two that he loved being a dad and wanted more kids."

He glanced up sharply, held her gaze. "You're not out of that game. You can always adopt."

Though she and her father had never come right out and talked about this, she wasn't surprised that he'd thought it through, that he'd already come to this conclusion. She smiled shakily. "I know."

"So what's the deal? Why can't we talk about him?"

"Because in spite of the fact that I knew we weren't a good match I sort of let myself fall." She sucked in a breath. "But I'm okay now. And I can tell you that he's definitely interested in the store. He has to talk to his family first."

"Maybe I don't want to sell it to him."

For the first time in hours, she laughed. "Don't cut off your nose to spite your face. The Wallaces own a big company, with lots of capital. I'm sure they'll make you a very fair offer."

"Everything in life isn't about money."

She laughed again, glowing with the fact that her dad loved her enough not to take a deal.

Even though that was idiotic and she planned to talk him out of it, she said, "That's the first time you've ever said that."

"Well, it's true." He scooted his chair closer to the table. "Are we going to eat tonight or what?"

His mom brought him a drink. "It's only a little after five. I invited Mary to dinner at seven. Have a drink, go get a shower, and before you know it Mary will be here."

A sudden knock at the door had her mom turning around. "Maybe she's early?"

"Maybe," Shannon said, heading out of the kitchen. "But, seriously, Dad, supper's not ready until seven. So you might as well get a shower."

With that she pushed through the swinging door and walked up the hall. She opened the door with a jolly "Merry Christmas," only to have Finley propel herself at her knees.

"Merry Christmas, Shannon!"

Shocked, she looked up at Rory. Their gazes caught. "Merry Christmas, Shannon."

Her heart tumbled in her chest. It was wonderful to see them. Fabulous that they were still in Pennsylvania this late. That probably meant they wanted to share Christmas with her.

But it was also bad because she'd finally, finally stopped crying and finally, finally reminded herself that she could adopt on her own.

Create the family she wanted. Seeing them again only brought back her sad sensations of loss.

"Can we come in?"

Shaking herself out of her stunned state, she said, "Yes. Yes, of course."

Her mom pushed open the kitchen door and came into the hall. Obviously expecting to see Mary, she frowned. "Oh, Mr. Wallace? What can we do for you?"

"Actually, I'd like to talk to Shannon."

Her mother's perfectly shaped brows arched in question.

Shannon said, "My dad is here. If you want to talk about the store..."

He caught her gaze again. "I want to talk to you. Privately."

Finley huffed out a sigh, walked to Shannon's mom. "That means he wants us to go." She caught Stacy's hand. "We can make cocoa."

Stacy laughed. "I'll give you five minutes. After that, I won't be responsible for what the kitchen looks like."

When the kitchen door swung closed behind them, Shannon stood staring it at. After a few seconds, Rory put his hands on her shoulders, turned her around.

"First, I'm sorry."

She shrunk back. "That's okay. I get it. You had to go." She smiled sheepishly. "I'm surprised you're here now. Isn't your family going to miss you?"

"My parents are in Arizona with my sister and her family for the holiday."

"Oh. So this will be good for Finley then—"

He tightened his hold on her shoulders. "Stop. I'm trying to tell you something here." He sucked in a breath. "I think I love you. I know it's crazy. We've known each other only a few days. But hear me out. We've both been hurt. So we're both smart about love. We don't give away our hearts frivolously, so for me to have lost mine, I know this has to be right. Now you can argue, but I—"

Catching his cheeks in her hands, Shannon rose to her tiptoes and pressed her mouth to his. She let the joy of following an impulse flow through her as she deepened the kiss, expressed every ounce of crazy feeling inside of her through one hot press of her mouth to his.

Then she pulled away, stared into his eyes and said the words she'd been aching to say for days. "I love you, too."

He grinned. "Really? In a few days? You don't think we're crazy?"

"Oh, we're definitely crazy, but that's okay."

She patted her chest with her right hand. "I know here that it's right."

"So you won't think it out of line for me to ask you to marry me?"

"I think it will go easier on us at the adoption agency if we're married."

He sucked in a breath. "So you won't mind adopting kids? Because I really do want to raise more kids."

"We can adopt seven if you want."

He laughed, caught her around the waist and hauled her to him. This time he kissed her. He let his tongue swirl around hers, nudged her so close that their hearts beat against each other. Savored the moment he knew, truly knew, that he loved her.

And that this time love would last.

Then he heard the swinging door open and he broke the kiss. Seeing Finley slinking into the foyer, he smiled down at Shannon and nudged his head in the direction of his daughter, alerting her to Finley's presence.

"So now that all that's settled, Finley would like to know how Santa gets all around the world in one night."

Her eyes widened in horror. "Seriously, you want me to field this?"

"I already tried and failed."

Smiling, Finley blinked at her expectantly.

She glanced up at him and he raised his eyebrows, letting her know he, too, was eager to hear what she said.

She stooped in front of Finley. "Santa's sleigh is powered by love."

Finley squinted. "Love?"

"It's the love of all the parents in the world that gets his sleigh to get to every house in one night."

Finley pondered that, but Rory's heart expanded. Leave it to Shannon to know exactly what to say. Was it any wonder he loved her?

Shannon glanced up at Rory and said, "Without love nothing really works." She looked back at Finley. "But with love, everything works." She hugged her tightly, then rose and wrapped her arms around Rory. "You do realize we have to sleep on the floor."

"Huh?"

"My parents get the bedroom. We get the sleeping bags—"

Finley let out a whoop of joy. "And I get the sofa!" She headed for the living room. "Let's turn on the fireplace. Oh, and the tree lights. We can have the tree lights on all night!"

Rory cast a confused look toward the living room. "Do you think she'll fall asleep long enough for me to grab the gifts I bought Thursday afternoon from the back of my trunk?"

Shannon laughed. "She better."

"Or?"

She nestled against him. "Or we won't get any snuggle time, either."

Rory said, "Ah." Then he bent his head and kissed her.

EPILOGUE

THE FOLLOWING Christmas Eve, Rory stood near the half wall of the mezzanine watching Finley play Santa's helper. Over the course of the year that had passed, she'd finally caught on to the whole Santa thing. Due in no small part to the new friends she'd made in Green Hill when he and Shannon had bought Mary O'Grady's house. She'd thought the place too big and decided she liked Shannon's house better, so they'd swapped. She took the little house that was remodeled. They got the old house and were in the process of redoing it to accommodate at least four kids.

Finley had discovered a little girl her age about a mile up the road and they'd had enough play dates that they behaved more like sisters than friends. Right now Finley and Gwen wore little green-and-red elf suits with red-and-green-striped tights. Each held a clipboard and pen.

They were the naughty and nice elves, writing down names. Finley kept track of the nice. Gwen was in charge of naughty. Funny thing was, Santa never put a kid on the naughty list. Only the nice.

Shaking his head, Rory laughed and glanced down at the first-floor sales floor. Hundreds of customers swarmed around tables and racks. The line at the candy department was six deep. Congratulating himself on the money they'd be making, he glanced at the door and straightened suddenly.

Shannon's parents had arrived. Early.

As if they had radar, they headed for the mezzanine steps. Within seconds, they were beside him.

"Hey, Rory!" Stacy hugged him.

"Rory." A bit more standoffish, Shannon's dad reluctantly offered his hand to shake his.

"I'm glad you're here early. You can see Finley in action."

Stacy glanced over. "Oh, she's adorable!"

Even Shannon's dad's expression softened a bit. "She's quite a kid."

"Due in no small part to your daughter," Rory said, desperately trying to make points with this guy, who still wasn't over the fact that Rory had left Christmas Eve the year before. Never mind that he'd come back and proposed marriage to his daughter even though they'd only known each other a week. Nope. Dave still held a grudge. "She's a wonderful mother. I couldn't raise Finley without her."

Stacy looked around. "Speaking of Shannon, where is she?"

He didn't know. She'd been missing in action all morning and he wasn't sure it was wise to tell her parents that. He hadn't lost her. She was a grown woman, allowed to go Christmas shopping on her own if she chose, but somehow he didn't think her dad would like that answer.

Still, he sucked in a breath, ready to say, "I'm not sure where she is," when he saw Shannon get off the elevator and stride toward him.

The happy expression on her face hit him right in the heart. He couldn't believe he'd almost walked away from her the year before.

She strode over, directly into his open arms. "Can I talk to you?"

He turned her to see that her parents were already there.

"Mom? Dad? You're early."

Her dad scowled. "Why, is that bad?"

"It's not bad, Dad. It's just that I have something to tell Rory."

Her dad harrumphed. "You can tell him in front of us…unless there's something wrong."

"Nothing wrong," Rory assured him, then prayed there wasn't.

Shannon cleared her throat. "Okay, then—" She slid her arm around Rory again. "I've spent the morning with the adoption agency." She turned in Rory's arms. "Melissa Graham had her baby. She chose us as the parents."

Rory's heart stopped. As he grabbed Shannon and hugged her, he noticed Shannon's parents' faces fall in disbelief. "We get a baby?"

Her eyes glowed. "A boy."

His breath stuttered out. "A boy."

She hugged him again. "A baby. Our baby boy."

The speakers above them began to play the hallelujah chorus. Shannon laughed. Rory bit back tears, not wanting Shannon's dad to see him cry.

Pulling out of his embrace, Shannon said, "Who gets to tell Finley that she's about to be a big sister?"

Rory turned her toward Santa's throne. He put his arm around Stacy's shoulders and tugged on Shannon's dad's arm. "Let's tell her together."

* * * * *